MW01595216

No part of this publication may be reproduced, stored in a retrieval system, or transmitted in any form or by any means, electronic, mechanical, photocopying, recording, scanning, or otherwise, without the prior written permission of the publisher, except in the case of brief quotations within critical reviews and otherwise as permitted by copyright law.

NOTE: This is a work of fiction. Names, characters, places, and incidents are a product of the author's imagination. Any resemblance to real life is purely coincidental. All characters in this story are 18 or older.

Copyright © 2016, Willow Winters Publishing. All rights reserved.

LOGAN
&
CHARLOTTE

WILLOW WINTERS &
LAUREN LANDISH
WALL STREET JOURNAL & USA TODAY BESTSELLING AUTHORS

From USA Today bestselling authors, Willow Winters and Lauren Landish, comes a seduction office romance.

I'm used to dominating the boardroom and getting what I want.
But I've never wanted anyone like her.
Even though I have the world at my beck and call,
it no longer excites me.
Nothing does., until she comes along.
My Rose.

Her deep blue eyes. Her tempting curves.
They call to me, consuming my thoughts like nothing has in years.
I should walk away,
but the soft sighs spilling from her plump lips are addictive.

I've never felt such desire.
I've never wanted like this.

I shouldn't fall this deep and I know it.
There's a reason I keep everyone away,
and I need to remember that.
But now that I have her in my grasp, I can't let her go.

Mr
CEO

PROLOGUE

LOGAN

She thinks I don't know what she's been doing.

My Rose.

She's been teasing me. Taunting me with those swaying hips and short skirts. Making my dick so hard it fucking hurts.

"Bend over." I give her the simple command and hold her heated gaze. She's a rebel at heart. She has no reason to obey me unless she wants to. And I fucking know she wants to. She wants *me,* just as much as I want her.

Her lips pull into a sexy smirk as her hands slowly fall onto the desk and she spreads her legs slightly before bending over. My dick instantly hardens in my pants. She looks over her shoulder at me with nothing but lust on her face.

"Like this?" she asks in a soft sweet voice, feigning innocence. She's not innocent at all. She practically begged for this.

Her skirt's slipped up past her upper thighs, and I can see her garter belt and the beautiful curve of her ass. I lower myself to the floor behind her. That's what she does to me. She makes me fall to my knees.

"Just like that," I murmur as I gentle my hands on her thighs.

I inch my fingers up, playing with the thin black straps. The tips of my fingers trace along her creamy thighs, leaving goosebumps in their path.

I lightly brush my hands along her panty line and I'm rewarded with a soft moan spilling from her plump lips. "You like that, Rose?" I ask her as I hook my fingers into the waistband of her lace thong.

I keep my eyes on hers as I slowly pull the skimpy lace thong down to the floor. Her mouth parts slightly and her eyes widen, but she doesn't stop me. I know I shouldn't be doing this. I shouldn't give in to the temptation and make this more complicated. But I'm a selfish man, and I want her.

I repress a groan as she slowly steps out of her thong and widens her stance for me.

"Yes, sir," she breathes out in a voice laced with desire, "I do." I can't help the asymmetric grin that pulls at my lips. I splay my hand on her lower back, just above those cute little dimples and push her down.

She's spread and fully bared to me, glistening with arousal.

"I wanna taste you," I say against her hot pussy before taking a languid lick. Her legs tremble in her high-as-fuck black leather heels and for a second I worry she won't be able to maintain her balance in them. But I wanna fuck her in them. Just like this, this is exactly how I want her. I've dreamed of this every day since the first day I laid eyes on her.

I need to get her good and ready for me.

I take my time forcing those sounds of pleasure from her lips. I lick my lips and groan at her sweet taste before flicking my tongue against her throbbing clit. Her back tries to arch off the desk, but I hold her down.

She's going to give me every fantasy I've ever dreamed of. I can't tell her the truth about me, and I know I shouldn't bring her into this, but her taste on my tongue and the soft sounds that spill from her gorgeous lips make me weak.

She moans my name, and it's my undoing.

I can't take it anymore. I stand and quickly unbutton my pants, shoving them down as quickly as I can. She turns her head to watch as she waits patiently, remaining in the position I left her in.

I kick my pants off carelessly with my eyes on hers and stand behind her with my hands gripping her hips. Her eyes are clouded with lust. Not the fear that used to be there. She trusts me. She wants me, and nothing's holding her back now. If only she knew the truth. I can never give her what she needs.

I know I'm selfish, but I'm taking her.

CHAPTER 1

LOGAN

The ice in the cognac glass clinks as the bartender sets it in front of me on the small white cocktail napkin. I give him a small nod and return my attention to the tablet in my hand. I'm not going to drink the whiskey I ordered. I'm not going to talk to anyone in here, although I'm sure a few business men will approach me. I'm simply waiting for my associate, Trent Morgan.

He's much more... sociable than I am. I prefer solitude. I do my best work in my office. And if it were any other day, that's where we'd be. On the top floor of the high-rise that encompasses the success of my company, Parker-Moore Enterprise. From the outside, the sixty-four story building looks as though it's one sheet of mirrored glass with symmetrical beveled lines that separate the floors.

I inherited the business, but the building is all mine. The idea and the structure. I get the credit for that. The massive influx of clients and and profits, they're all me, too.

And I didn't get there by holding meetings at a bar in the Madison Hotel.

Dozens of men and women are lingering around me. Some at the high top tables near the large floor-to-ceiling windows that look over the edge and onto the crystal clear harbor below. It's breathtaking, and at one point in my life I may have enjoyed this room, but right now I'm irritated.

I look back to my tablet, to the one thing I have a vested interest in, my work, and ignore the hum of small talk and the faint sounds of laughter from the other side of the room. There are two companies I'm interested in. They're the reason I'm sitting here. On paper, they're nearly identical. I want to see the *people*. They'll tell me which of the two is worth investing in. People run a business, and if I can't have faith in the men and women heading the company, then I have no interest in investing.

I glance up as a small, delicate hand gently brushes my forearm. Her thin fingers and glossy red nail polish make her hand look extra dainty resting easily on my dark grey custom-tailored Armani suit. I clear my throat and turn my head slightly to look at the woman who takes a graceful seat on the barstool next to me.

It takes great effort not to stare at the cleavage she's obviously put on display. Her form-fitting black dress has a plunging neckline, with a sharp "V" that travels too far down to be professional.

She practically purrs, "I was hoping you'd buy me a drink."

I huff a small laugh and smirk at her. That's a cheeky come-on I wasn't expecting and I can appreciate her charm; the drinks are free for the conference. And I can tell from the soft blush across her cheeks and the sweet grin on her lips that she already knows that.

She's beautiful and refined. Her confidence is alluring, but it does nothing for me.

"I'm waiting on a colleague." I'm short in my response for a reason. I don't want to open doors for discussion.

If we'd met in this scenario three years ago, things would be different. I'd have taken her upstairs to my bed in the penthouse suite and given her what she's looking for. I wouldn't have thought twice about it. I would've satisfied the both of us and moved on to the next sweet little thing looking to sink her claws into a wealthy man.

Things change. People change.

I have no room in my life for complications anymore. I don't mix business with pleasure. I lead a private life for good reason. And if my parents' failed marriage and brutal divorce taught me anything, it's that I should never trust anyone.

And I can't afford to let anyone in. Not now. Not ever.

The little minx gives me a tight smile and gathers her clutch in a white-knuckled fist before sliding off the barstool. I don't mind her disgruntled departure. I'm used to it, and I prefer it that way. I could apologize for being blunt and to the point, but I'm not sorry. And I don't make apologies.

There are only two people in this world I'm close to. My father, and the man who just walked into the room, Trent Morgan. He cocks a brow and watches the woman pull her dress down a bit more as she gives me the cold shoulder and stalks off without a word.

A sly grin forms on his cleanly shaven face as he takes her seat and looks at me. "Already pissing people off. You couldn't wait for me to start the party, could you?"

I let out a deep rough chuckle. I've always liked Trent. He's nearly a decade older than me as he approaches forty, but we've gotten along since day one. Which isn't the case for most Parker-Moore executives.

I've always taken this business seriously. After seeing my mother shred my father after his stroke and try to steal the business out from under him, I knew anyone and everyone who thought they could try to take it from me would. And I was ready for them.

I'm not sure if Trent liked the fact that I was ruthless in business and didn't trust anyone even at such a young age, or if he was just relieved that his new twenty-two-year-old boss wasn't some spoiled brat who didn't give a fuck about the business he'd just inherited.

But seven years later, he's my closest ally. He's my *only* ally.

He signals to the bartender for a drink before looking down the bar at mine. "I'll take care of that for you," he says as he picks up the glass. The napkin sticks to the bottom as he brings it to his lips and downs the drink in a single swig.

"Stressed?" I ask him with a cocky grin.

"I am," he answers without looking at me. I know why he's anxious, I'm just waiting for him to say it. He smiles at the bartender as he orders another Jack on ice. I got him hooked on my drink of choice. He turns to face me before he says, "We need to choose, and neither of them look like they can handle our influx."

He has a right to be upset. We bit off more than we can chew. We have the manufacturing capabilities, but the sales just aren't there. Hiring out isn't paying off like it should. "Our profits are shit for the retail division," Trent says, accepting his drink and taking a modest sip.

"I'm aware," I say and nod, rapping my knuckles on the bar, "and that's a fixable problem."

He looks at me from the corner of his eye. "You're more laidback about this than you should be."

I shrug. I may be a little less stressed than normal over this, but it's because this has happened before. "For every problem, there's a solution," I say easily.

"I imagine that means you got good news on Thursday?" he asks. My body tenses, and I don't answer. Instead I face the bartender and wait for him to make eye contact with me.

I'm vaguely aware of Trent apologizing as I hear a small feminine voice to my left. It catches me off guard for some reason, and I turn and see a beautiful short woman with sun-kissed skin and gorgeous blonde hair.

She gives the bartender a small smile, but it's merely to be polite. Her brilliant blue eyes are dimmed by something. In a room full of people, she stands out. She's like me in that she doesn't belong here. But I'm not sure why.

I watch her body language and see how closed off she is. She's uncomfortable. A small sigh leaves her plush lips as she sits back at the bar with her eyes closed. The sight makes my dick instantly harden. She looks vulnerable and beautiful. She looks tempting in so many ways.

The sound of her giving in, that soft sigh--I want that. I want to hear it again and again. Even more than that though, I want to force those sounds from her lips myself.

CHAPTER 2

CHARLOTTE

Y*our shit better be gone by the time I'm back!*

My last words to my ex run through my mind as I step into
the Madison Hotel bar. I stop for a moment to address my
outfit, a black pencil skirt with a shiny belt wrapped around
my waist, giving my figure a shapely appearance, and a pearly
white blouse. I scan the room, noting it's filled to the brim
with business people, and wonder if I should head back out
into the lobby to collect myself. This is a business convention
and I need to be on my A game. But I didn't come down to
the bar for business.

I'm supposed to be focused on this presentation and

making contacts, but all I can think about is what happened. What *they* did to me.

Even now the pain is razor sharp, cutting me deep.

I turn to leave the bar, but then stop.

I can't go back, I tell myself. *I refuse to go back to crying over people who aren't worth an ounce of my time.*

It's easy to tell myself this, but harder to put it in action. The betrayal has been a difficult thing to swallow. Especially considering the source of my agony.

Sarah was once a good friend to me, a co-worker and confidante that I thought had my best interests at heart. Turns out her only interest was getting my boyfriend's cock out of his boxers and into her lying mouth.

Ian's infidelity had been bad enough, but Sarah's disloyalty was deeply personal. I'd trusted her, and with everything. The way she played up to me all that time, giving me advice on everything from my hair, makeup, outfits and my relationship with Ian, only to stab me in the back when the first opportunity arrived--makes my blood fucking boil.

Screw her, I think to myself angrily. *And screw him. They both deserve each other. I'm here now, and it's time to move on with my life.* The wounds are only a little over a week old, but I'm tired of wallowing in grief. It's useless. And I can't let anything ruin this job for me. I couldn't stand being near that bitch so I left in the heat of the moment. Not the smartest thing I've ever done. But I still managed to get a good recommendation and land this job quickly. Thankfully.

Deciding it's time to drink my worries away, I head over to the bar. The clicking of my heels from the hallway is muted by the thin carpet in the lounge area. I grab an end seat in a leather wingback chair, loving the open yet cozy vibe of the room and signal the bartender, a young blond man dressed in a black tux; he's quick to make his way over.

"What will you have, sweetie?" His voice has a high-pitched note to it.

I give him a friendly smile in return. He's handsome and all, but definitely batting for the other team. "Apple martini, please," I reply.

He winks at me. "You got it."

I watch as he leaves me.

Everything's going to be fine. Just watch.

I'm just starting to feel more relaxed when I feel eyes boring into the back of my neck. I look around, and then my breath catches in my throat.

Holy hell, I think to myself, my eyes widening slightly.

A man seated at the bar just a few feet away is blatantly staring at me. Not just any man. The perfect mix of CEO and sex god. I can see he's wearing a crisp white dress shirt with only the top button undone under his suit, and his dark hair is slightly messy on top. He looks like he'd pin your legs back and take what he wanted from you.

My breath catches in my throat. He's so fucking

handsome. There's no way he was looking at me. No way in hell. He's way out of my league. His suit looks high dollar, and he's groomed to perfection. Even the air around him is too expensive for me.

The bartender startles me as he comes back with my drink, and I break my eye contact with the mystery man. I give the bartender a nervous smile and wiggle the thin cocktail pick with a bit of apple on it around in the glass, my heart pounding in my chest. *Jesus.* I feel like I'm having hot flashes. I have to wonder though, if that guy can do this to me with just a look, what could he do with a single touch?

I can't help myself. I have to look back over. I chance a quick peek. *Shit.* He's still looking right at me. I jerk my eyes away with my breath stilling in my lungs. Holy shit. He *is* looking at me. His light blue eyes pierce into me this time, holding my gaze. My lips part slightly as the feeling of being trapped washes over me. My body tenses. He's intense. *Too intense.* Luckily a man to his right taps his shoulder and Mr. CEO turns to face him with a look of annoyance.

I take that as my cue to get the hell out of here while I can. *He* is a bad idea. And I need to stay far away.

I abandon my drink, nearly spilling it on the table as I set it down as quickly as I can along with a twenty from my purse. I grab my black leather Coach hobo with both hands, my eyes focused on the open entryway. My skin flushes as I pass him, making my exit a little too quickly to go unnoticed.

I don't even breathe until I'm on the elevator and the doors are closing. I stand there feeling overwhelmed and not even realizing that I need to hit the button to get this thing moving.

I need to get a grip. I push the button for my floor and lean back against the wall of the empty cart. A waist-high bar is behind me and I hold it to steady myself. What the hell was that about? I replay the scene in my head, but there's no way I'm remembering it right.

The way he looked at me triggered something deep inside me; something I've never felt before. A mix of fear and lust.

It was like he owned me.

CHAPTER 3

LOGAN

The curtains are open in the penthouse suite, but the soft glow from the harbor outside does nothing to brighten the darkness in the room. It doesn't matter. The dim light from my laptop is all I need. I'm used to it. I'm most productive at night.

This is the ideal atmosphere for me, but I can't focus. I've been staring at the same portfolio since I came up here and took my seat at the corner desk in my hotel room. My fingers tap against the smooth surface of the hard maple desk in a soothing beat.

I can't calm down though. I'm nothing but tense and anxious. I want something I can't have, and that's a rarity.

She's someone I shouldn't pursue. I already know this,

yet I'm toying with the idea of making her mine. There's a difference between finding a quick fuck to ease my appetite and taking with the intention of keeping her.

And I already know once won't be enough.

What's worse is that I know keeping her entails a sort of relationship. One I'm not inclined to have. A fuck buddy is an impossibility for me. I've learned that the hard way. Women lie. I don't know whether they're lying to themselves or just to me, but when they say they're happy with only being my fucktoy, they're lying. Even if I'm paying them. They always want more.

I don't know what came over me downstairs and even now. I can't get her out of my thoughts. I shouldn't even be considering this knowing what she'll be getting in return.

I want her though, and I haven't ever wanted someone like this before. I wish she were here now, and I keep picturing it over and over. I want her straddling me, with her shapely legs draped on either side of mine and her arms wrapped around my neck.

My cock hardens in my pants. I can hear those soft moans as I fist her hair at the nape of her neck and thrust my dick over and over into her hot, tight cunt. I lean back in my seat and sigh as I try to erase the image from my head.

I've sworn off companionship. I don't need it. But something about her is drawing me in. Insta-lust at its finest. I haven't fallen victim to that in quite a while.

I don't need anyone. And it's best I don't get attached.

More so for them than for me.

I'm a selfish man, but I'm not so selfish that I'd bring another person into my life. There's a reason I keep them away.

I need to remember that.

I can't have her; I'm firm in that decision. But even as I come to that conclusion, I find myself looking through the convention's website. I just need to know her name. With a little digging I'm certain I'll lose interest in her. I'm sure it's the fact that she left before I could talk to her, leaving me wanting, that has the image of her branded in my consciousness. At least that's what I tell myself to justify looking through the list of presenters with their square pictures and short biographies.

I fucking want her.

As the thought hits me, her picture appears on the screen. My fingers stop on the touchpad as I take in the soft curves of her face. Her beautiful smile puts my memory to shame.

Charlotte Rose Harrison.

I focus on her middle name Rose, which is also the color of her lips, and the delicate features fit her perfectly. She was meant to be a Rose.

Keynote speaker for Armcorp and former executive of sales for Steamens Marketing.

Education: Graduated from North State University (2013) with master's degrees in business, marketing and economics.

I've seen resumes like this before. Although I have to admit her progression in a mere three years is impressive. I'm not concerned with her work habits though. I should be, but in this very moment, I don't give a fuck about any of that. I want to know about *her*.

I open a new browser tab and type in her name.

Specifically, I want to know who she's fucking. That's the only thing on my mind.

Before I can press enter, I shut the laptop with more force than what's needed and slowly rise from my seat, shaking my head.

Now's not the time or place for this shit. This is business. And she could be an employee of mine if we settle on her company. It's one of the two we're considering.

I stalk across the room in darkness and head to the large windows.

The idea of buying Armcorp just to be close to her eases the part of me that's panicking to act now before she slips through my fingers. If she's close, I can keep tabs on her until my interest wanes. And I'm sure it will.

I run my hand through my hair and then lean against the window. It feels cool against the palms of my hands.

It's an easy enough decision to make. A shit reason to make a business decision, but I don't need anyone's approval. I own my business, and I can do whatever the fuck I want to do with it.

I close my eyes and lean my forehead against the cold glass. It's late and I can't be rash in this decision. My hands ball into fists as I push off the large window and move to the king-size bed in the room.

Tomorrow I'll decide. Either I'm taking her, or I'll leave her and this fantasy alone. As I close my eyes my dick begins hardening with the thoughts of what I want to do with her and I already know what my decision will be.

Charlotte *Rose* is *mine*.

CHAPTER 4

CHARLOTTE

T*he pressure is real.*

Convention hall. Game face on.

I'm sitting in the audience filled with my peers, coworkers and powerful business executives, trying to calm my rising anxiety. A lot is riding on this presentation. It could literally be the difference between having a job, or being on the street. Armcorp just hired me, and if I don't ace this I know they'll be wondering if I'm worth it.

To make matters worse, my boss is sitting right behind me and he'll see everything. I'm doing my best to stay still and not appear nervous. I hold my head upright and do my best to project confidence, even though I'm drowning with anxiety inside. I hope he can't sense that I'm nearly having a panic attack right beneath his nose.

I can do this, I tell myself. *I'm strong, smart and confident. I have this presentation memorized. This is what I do, and I'm damn good at it.*

I keep repeating these words in my mind, letting it become a powerful mantra that drives back the anxiety that threatens to send me running from the room a nervous wreck.

I will succeed. There's nothing I can't do. They hired me because they were impressed by my resume and experience. I have absolutely nothing to worry about.

I obsessively click on my phone and look at the time. Each presentation is fifteen minutes long and I'm up next. Two minutes left. *Shit.* My heart won't stop racing. I dim my cell's screen and put my phone away.

I don't know what I'm going to do when I'm called up on that stage. I'm practically shaking like a leaf.

A soft voice interrupts my anxious thoughts.

"You're going to do fine," Eva White, a coworker who's sitting right next to me, says. I look over and she's staring at me with empathy, her large brown eyes looking at me reassuringly. For a moment, I feel my anxiety ease and I'm grateful that she's sitting next to me.

Like me, she's dressed to impress, in a sleek black pantsuit with her dark red hair pulled back into a professional ponytail.

I smile back at her, unease twisting my stomach, and

mouth, *thank you*.

"You're welcome." She gently pats me on the leg to comfort me and I'm reminded of her nickname. *Sweet Eva*. I'm so lucky to call her a friend. In the corporate world, there's no shortage of people who will backstab you in the blink of an eye to climb the ladder, but not Eva. She's a team player, and it's one of the reasons I trust her already. When we're together, shit gets done.

The announcer walks back up on stage to the podium as the previous presenter leaves, and despite my mental pep talk and Eva's reassurance, my heart begins doing backflips and sweat slicks my palms.

"And now," he says into the microphone, "I'd like to introduce the keynote speaker presenting Armcorp's quarterly report, Miss Charlotte Rose Harrison."

Oh my God. I'm so fucked.

Polite applause floods my senses and I climb to my feet with a tight smile on my face.

You'll do fine, Eva mouths to me.

I give her a thankful smile despite the butterflies fluttering in my stomach.

I make my way to the front of the room as quickly as I can without falling on my face in these heels, my heart beating wildly with every step. I'm careful not to trip as I climb the steps to the stage and walk over to the podium. The announcer hands me a small clicker to control the projector behind me. I glance up and see the powerpoint I prepared. My heart races as I square my shoulders and straighten my back.

Alright, Charlotte. You can't fuck this up.

For a moment I'm blinded by the bright lights on the stage making me the center of attention in the darkened room. I can't view the sea of executives in the audience or anything for a moment. It's just me and the stage with the projector behind me.

Slowly, everyone comes back into focus. I can see them all. Faces I know, some that I don't. They're all waiting for me. Staring. I swear I'm starting to sweat in places I didn't think I could. The pressure is immense.

Get on with it, girl! I can do this.

I swallow, and then take a deep breath. The lights are shining on me, waiting. My voice is caught in my throat, suffocated by nerves. But I take another deep breath and begin what I've rehearsed. It's almost like white noise in my ears as I rattle off the background and current state of Armcorp's hold on the market. I know these lines by heart.

I turn to the projected slides and click the small button to move forward. Everyone's watching. My blood heats and my heart races, but I know this. I quickly hit through all my notes and bullet points with an ease in my voice that doesn't reflect my nerves, and the more I talk, the more my confidence grows. This is how it is every time. I can barely handle the pressure, and it's huge, but I'm damn good at pushing through and maintaining the professional presentation that's expected.

"So as you can see, the company's market share is growing by seventeen percent and it's on an upward trend," I say, turning around to face the room of corporate executives. They're all watching and judging me. And they should be; this is business, after all. "By reaching out to the other markets depicted in table five of this slide we anticipate a growth-" I pause as my eyes lock with the handsome stranger from the bar last night, my ability to speak momentarily stolen. The lines I've rehearsed seem to vanish and not a word can pass the lump in my throat.

He's sitting in the back of the room, watching me with an intense gaze that makes me feel like I'm sitting in a 120 degree sauna.

Jesus. Focus, Charlie!

I clear my throat and open my mouth to continue. But nothing comes out. My mind's blank. I stand there for several moments, my heart pounding. I need to get myself together. The corner of Mr. CEO's lips rise in an asymmetric grin as he stares at me. He's affecting me, and he knows it. Suddenly, I'm pissed. My nerves shift and anger replaces them. Nothing's going to stop me from acing this and proving to everyone that I'm damn good at what I do and that I'm worth it.

I tear my eyes away from him, trying to unscramble my thoughts. A few attendees shift in their seats. They're probably thinking I've suddenly gone brain-dead.

I turn my back on the room and face the drawing board, pointing with the tiny light in the clicker at the projection screen. Even with my body breaking out into a cold sweat, I push forward, quickly thinking on my toes until I'm able to remember my presentation. "And so what we have here..." As I point my wand at the graph, my hands start to tremble.

"Is room for exponential growth," I continue on smoothly with my presentation as if nothing happened, even though it feels like my heart is climbing up my throat. I get through the next few minutes, presenting data clearly and easily. By the time I'm done, I'm covered with a sheen of sweat. But I'm sure I've done a competent job.

"And we will grow our profit margin by nearly ninety percent," I say, turning to face the room in conclusion. I smile brightly and signal to the announcer that I'm done. Looking at the large clock on the far back wall, I see I've hit the fifteen minute mark right on the dot. *Perfect.* "Thank you for having me." The room bursts into a scattering of light applause. I beam with relief although I'm still hot as hell with anxiety. Both from the presentation and from *him.*

My nerves are still high, but I feel a slight sense of relief. I did it. It's over, and other than that hiccup it went just as I planned. No thanks to Mr. CEO. I start to look his way but then stop. I'm not going to give him the satisfaction. He almost ruined my presentation.

I make my way back to my seat as the announcer walks up

to introduce the next speaker, being careful again not to trip in my heels. That would be embarrassing as fuck.

I wiggle my way through the row and back to my seat next to Eva. She's looking at me with admiration as I sit down.

"See, what did I tell you?" she squeals in a hushed voice, pulling me into a soft embrace. "You did fantastic!"

"Thank you," I whisper back. "I couldn't have done it without you."

Eva waves her hand as she releases me from our hug. "Nonsense. You had that in the bag before you even stepped foot on the stage. Hell, I wish I could speak like that in front of a large crowd. You're a natural."

"Job well done, Charlotte," my new boss, Charles Hastings, chips in from behind me. I turn to face him with a grateful smile as he places a hand on my shoulder. Charles's an older man in his forties with dark hair, greying at the temples, and a chiseled jawline that is beginning to lose its strength. He's the type of man I'd be attracted to if I were into older guys. Or if I was about five years older, he definitely could get it. Except he doesn't hold a candle to...

I try to push Mr. CEO out of my thoughts, but it doesn't work. All I can see is his handsome face in my mind's eye, his piercing gaze, his crisp suit and his full lips. All I can think about is how much I want to kiss them. Good God.

"Thank you, sir," I say, trying to shake the man from my mind.

"No, thank you, Charlotte," Charles tells me, patting me

on the shoulder. "That was a wonderful presentation. You made our company look good."

Seeing as how I was about to pass out from anxiety before taking the stage, I should be overjoyed that I'm getting such praise from my boss. But I can't fight the urge to look over for the stranger.

My heart does a little jolt. His seat is empty. He's gone.

I settle back in my seat feeling a pang of disappointment.

I try to focus on the next speaker as the slides change on the screen in front of us. But I can't concentrate. I can't shake the hold he has over me. And why? Why does he have such a strong effect on me?

I can't tame the urge to look back over my shoulder. He's not there. I swallow thickly and try to ignore all thoughts of him. I don't even know his name.

But I want to. I'm woman enough to admit that I'm at least curious.

CHAPTER 5

LOGAN

"Why this one?" Trent asks me again. He's been eyeing me since we sat down in the meeting room.

I settle back in the seat although it's extremely uncomfortable and try to relax. I can't wait to get out of here and take this damn jacket off. I feel restless now that I've made my decision. I have to wait and that's something I'm not fond of. Patience has never been my strong suit. And I need this deal. I never *need* anything, but right now I do. Armcorp had better take my offer.

"It's the best choice," I answer simply, not giving anything away. He gives me a look laced with suspicion but closes his mouth and looks back down at the papers in front of him.

I take a long look around the plain hotel meeting room with distaste as I wait for the heads of Armcorp to arrive.

This room is small and the large table that nearly takes up the entire space and the chairs surrounding it are cheap. It's nothing like the suite upstairs or my office back at Parker-Moore. I practically live there and I made sure it had every amenity I'd need. But this small square room... it's lacking. The walls are a stark white and the thin carpet on the floors makes it feel even more inferior. I'm ready to go back to the comfort of my own building and business, and I've decided I'm taking my Rose as a parting gift.

"Armcorp looks like a ton of work. We should give them a year or two to see how well their new outreach performs." Trent's right, and I can't deny that. But I'm not waiting. I've made up my mind.

Watching her on stage created more conflict than I needed. She's graceful and intelligent. But when we locked eyes and I felt the intensity of the spark between us, I knew I had to give in. She sealed her fate when her lips parted and she got lost in my trance. It's one thing for me to be affected, but knowing I do the same for her makes this decision easy.

"We should wait, Logan. The board will-" I don't care what argument he has. In fact, I know there are good reasons to wait or to go with their competitor. But I don't give a damn. I'm not waiting anymore. I fucking want her, and I'm not going to deny myself. I don't give a damn if I'm selfish.

I'm taking her. And this is the first step.

"No, I want it now." My voice is hard and the trace of annoyance causes Trent to flinch. I clench my jaw, wishing I could control myself. I need to. I pride myself on discipline, but when it comes to her, I feel like I'm losing it. Once I have her under my thumb, it will be easier.

Trent doesn't say anything in return. He leans back in his seat and nods his head. Although I consider him a friend and I'm grateful for his advice when it comes to running this company, I'm the CEO and sole proprietor; what I want, I get.

As the thought registers, the door to the meeting room opens and we rise to stand from the cheap seats. I button my suit jacket and wait at the head of the table for Armcorp's CEO, Scott Nathaniel Murphy. He's accompanied by the head executive of sales, Mr. Hastings, and another man I don't recognize; he has a pad of paper and a pen in his hand so I'm assuming he's a secretary.

"Good morning, gentlemen," Murphy addresses us with a firm handshake. He places his other hand on top of mine as our hands clasp and looks me in the eyes. He's an older man and set in traditional ways. I admire that, at times. I give him a tight smile and take the head seat. I'm the first to sit, but the other men quickly follow suit.

"Thank you for attending this meeting on such short notice, gentlemen," I say and clear my throat and prepare for a hopefully quick and agreeable contract.

"The pleasure is ours, Mr. Parker." Murphy angles his seat slightly and says, "I was surprised to hear your offer is for silent partnership?" He says it as though it's a question. I'm not interested in dismantling the business. I merely want control over it so I can use their sales division for my own benefits.

I nod my head slightly and reply, "It would certainly benefit us both... immensely."

All the men nod their heads slightly in response, with the exception of Trent. There's no hint of his usual smile on his face. The sight makes the corner of my lips itch to turn up into a smile, but I resist. This is business.

I clear my throat and begin to say, "Let's get to the point and make this as easy a transaction as possible-"

Before I can finish, Murphy interrupts me by saying, "You'll need to come up in price then." I'm not used to being cut off, and I don't fucking like it. But I'm more than willing to get right to the point. I'm also not surprised. In the proposal, I put in an extremely low bid, not so much that it would be insulting, but low enough that I have plenty of room to make a guaranteed profit. I'm the only buyer, so I can offer whatever the fuck I want.

"We had almost four million in revenue last year, and that's only increasing." I hold Murphy's gaze as he does his best to give me a hard sell. I don't care about this shit. I know his company inside and out, what I want is his counter offer.

"Revenue isn't profit," Trent says, speaking up for the first

time. And it's a very good point, but again, I couldn't care less.

"Our return on investment last year was nearly two hundred percent," Hastings says as he sits forward in his seat. His suit already looks wrinkled from his posture. He steeples his fingers and continues, "The evaluation of the company two years ago didn't account for our growing sectors. We've outgrown expectations while maintaining our cash flow."

"That's an excellent indication of budgeting, but that's not what we're discussing," Trent says with a hard voice.

"Our profit margin is-"

"Minimal," Trent interjects. He barely says the word, but it's enough to stop Murphy in his sales pitch.

I keep my shoulders squared and stare straight ahead, unaffected by the tense air between Trent and Murphy. I will say it's a nice change of pace for Trent to be the one heading the negotiation. Usually I'm the one who comes out looking like an asshole. Not that I matter much. It's business. Always. I never take it personal, even if they do.

"A price?" I ask. It's all I want. And frankly, I'm so anxious to ensure I have my Rose under my thumb that I need to be careful and not agree to the first number he spits out.

Murphy straightens his tie and shifts slightly in his seat. Finally, he gives me the answer I've been waiting for and says, "The board won't settle for anything less than sixty million."

They don't even know their own worth. This is going better than I could've hoped.

Trent sits back in his seat and then looks at me. I can feel his gaze on me, but I ignore it. It's the *we've won* look. I can practically hear him screaming, *Take the deal!*

"We'll settle on fifty-five and your entire operations will relocate immediately. There's a floor that's prepared to accommodate your current staff and needs although it will need to be outfitted as the two of you see fit."

I know the offer is lower than what he asked, but not by much. It's a shit ton lower than what I anticipated paying. I could give him the sixty mil he asked for, but the old man is bluffing. No one in this business gives a bottom line price on the first offer. No one.

"And the cost of the outfitting?" Murphy asks with a raised brow. I resist the pull at the corner of my lips to smile. I know I've got him.

"Company expenses--of course, *my* company expenses." He purses his lips and looks at Hastings.

"Do we have a deal?" I ask in an even tone. My face is neutral. I keep it that way for a reason. No emotions in business.

Murphy gives me a broad smile as he says, "We have a deal, Mr. Parker." He reaches his hand out and I easily give him a firm handshake with my other hand on top of his. I finally allow the grin to show. *She's mine.*

"You'll have the files faxed to you in the morning, and I'll see you on Monday." I finally give him a nod as I rise from the table.

"Pleasure doing business with you Mr. Parker," he says,

releasing me from the firm handshake.

I force the smile to stay put and reply, "The pleasure is all mine."

Trent follows my lead as I make for the door, leaving everyone else to do whatever the hell they want.

A sense of ease settles through me at the thought of Rose and knowing she'll be in my building in only a few short days. That's too long to wait, but it's the best I can do in terms of business. For now, I'll need to be patient and that may be a challenge. If anything, I can find her here and buy her a drink. I remember the way she looked the first night at the bar, the way she bolted.

A smile slips into place as I realize she won't be able to do that now. I've got her now.

Trent gives me a hard smack on the back as we walk out of the room.

"You're a shark, Logan," he says with a smile. I huff a small laugh and try to push down the anxiety and unsettling feelings that are threatening to consume me. If only he knew my real reason. That would wipe the smile off his face.

Chapter 6

Charlotte

"I'm gonna fuck five hot guys tonight," Hannah, one of my new coworkers, announces as she grins and leans back in the seat. She's tipsy and happy and just joking around. And it's infectious. She laughs as she fixes the straps of her black clubbing dress. I swear her D-cup boobs are about to pop out. But maybe that's what she wants. "It's five or bust!"

We're driving in a corporate stretch limo up the Las Vegas strip. The girls--Eva, Hannah and Cary Ann--want to hit a couple of casinos and a few clubs before returning to our hotel rooms to retire for the night. I'm not sure I want to be a part of the excursion, but Eva convinced me to join in on the fun to keep up with appearances.

As the new girl, she didn't want me to seem like a Debbie Downer to the others.

I wasn't sure what to expect when we all piled into the limo, but I found myself quickly relaxing when I realized the other girls had quite the sense of humor. All of them seem down to earth and don't take themselves seriously, which is a good thing. It makes fitting in with them easier.

Cary Ann, a petite blonde with platinum highlights, frowns. She's seated across from me and is wearing a purple dress that is far too short, the hem rising so far up her legs that I think I can almost see her uterus. Cary jokes, "Only five? Why not make it ten?"

"Yeah," adds Eva. She's sitting next to me and she's looking pretty hot in her red-hot halter dress and her dark red hair pulled into a sleek ponytail, if I say so myself. Her makeup is flawless and her eyes, which are framed by dark mascara and liner, look bigger than usual. "It's Vegas, chica. Go big or go home."

Hannah bites her lower lip, twisting her face into a serious expression. "I don't know, guys. I'd definitely do ten guys if I could... but..." She trails off and shakes her head morosely.

"But what?" Cary Ann demands, leaning forward as the limo goes over a speed bump and we all jolt to the side.

Hannah pauses for a long moment before breaking out into a wide grin and howls, "I don't know if I have enough holes!"

The girls scream with laughter. Even I have to join in. I

really need a good laugh and a fun time after all the stress I've been through these last two weeks. The fucking breakup. The pressure from the presentation. The feeling of dread I feel about returning home and finding my boyfriend hasn't moved out yet. Or worse, finding him shacked up in bed with Sarah.

I really need to just unwind and relax so I don't have a nervous breakdown.

Despite Hannah's rowdy boast, I know this group isn't serious about hooking up with anyone tonight. Most likely, we'll all have a couple drinks, flirt a little, *maybe*, and return to our rooms tipsy a few dollars richer or poorer.

I know I won't be getting any action, I tell myself. *That's for damn sure.*

"There'll be none of that over here," Eva says, doing a swirling motion with her hand around her lady bits.

Hannah frowns, messing with her bra. I swear her right boob almost popped out. I have to put my hand between my legs to keep from reaching over and pulling up the neckline of her dress. "Why's that?"

Eva raises her head and says haughtily, "Because I have a loving boyfriend who can't wait for me to get back home."

Cary Ann snorts and drunkenly blurts out, "Please, he's probably at home banging his side chick in your bed right now!"

"Okay!" Hannah reaches across her seat to high five Cary Ann, nearly popping out of her dress in the process, and the two girls burst into giggles. "You know what they say; a man is only as faithful as his options!"

Eva grimaces and glances over at me. I know what she's thinking. And she's right. The joke makes me feel like shit.

Cary Ann pauses when she sees we aren't laughing. "Did I say something wrong?"

I can't respond. My throat is tight with emotion.

Eva comes to my rescue. "Charlotte's going through a breakup," she says quietly. Fuck, I hate this. I feel so damn uncomfortable.

Cary Ann's face crumples into a frown and she reaches across the limo to place a consolatory hand on mine. "Oh honey, I'm sorry. I didn't mean to upset you."

Tears burn my eyes and I swallow the lump in my throat. "It's okay."

"You sure?" asks Hannah. "I hate to think that we upset you."

"I'm fine," I lie, putting on a fake smile. "Really, you guys don't have to walk on eggshells around me." I wave it off.

"Okay, sorry," Cary Ann repeats. I can tell she's really mortified that she's caused me unintentional pain.

"Don't sweat it." I look around and ask, "So what are you guys having to drink when we get to the club?" I want to change the subject and get the focus off me. As soon as fucking possible.

Hannah claps her hands together, causing her boobs to jiggle. "A bahama mama! 'Cause I'm a big, hot mama."

"The walking dead!" Cary Ann squeals. "'Cause it's my

favorite show!"

"A blue Hawaii," says Eva, "my favorite."

There's a moment of silence and the girls look at me expectantly.

"Bloody Mary," I say, thinking quickly on my feet. *Because I want to fucking murder Ian.*

"Let's hit Surrender first," Cary suggests as the limo slows and we climb out. "I hear it's awesome."

"Hell yeah," says Hannah. "I'm game."

We make our way inside and I'm immediately enveloped by a pleasant tropical smell and the sounds of slots machine. It's so bright, I have to blink a couple of times to adjust.

The noises, the lights, the flood of people, it's all overwhelming. Sin City. This definitely looks like a place made for sin. I walk behind the ladies as they stride confidently to wherever they're taking me. They've been here before and they're acting like they own the place. I do my best to do the same and look like I belong.

I take my seat next to Eva and put my clutch on the bartop, taking another look around. This place is overwhelming.

I start to ask Eva how many times she's been here, but before I can even get a word out, she's holding her finger up and reaching in her purse for her buzzing phone.

She snatches it out and taps the screen. "Hold on a min," she says, turning her back and typing out a text. Damn. She's acting like whatever she's typing is top secret, her fingers flying across the touch screen like a roadrunner.

I used to do that, I think sadly and a surge of loneliness washes over me. *When Ian used to text me, I acted like it was the most important thing in the world to text back immediately.*

"It's Kevin," Eva says when she's done, confirming my suspicion.

I nod and force a smile as I watch Eva slip her phone back into her purse without a worry. "How's he doing?"

"Alright," Eva replies, "but he misses me." My heart clenches in my chest, but I keep the smile plastered on my face. "He hates when I'm away on business trips."

I nod and say a silent prayer of thanks as the bartender comes over and interrupts us. I order a long island iced tea in place of that Bloody Mary so I can get trashed. I'm not messing around tonight. At this point I need something strong.

Eva joins in with the other girls who are gossiping about someone who works for another company now. Someone I don't know.

I nurse my drink and try to keep up and chime in, but I have no clue who and what they're talking about. After a few minutes, their conversation seems to turn to white noise and I find myself staring into my drink, moving the ice around with the straw and wondering why I'm in such a horrible fucking mood.

Hannah and Cary Ann get up, causing me to snap out of it, and announce they're going to go *dance their tits off.* I have to cover my mouth as the guy at the end of the bar looks over at the two of them with a raised brow.

My smile instantly falls as Eva grabs me by the hand and pulls me off my barstool. I resist a little and say, "Seriously, no one wants to see me dance." I haven't had nearly enough alcohol to embarrass myself that much.

"Come on!" She tugs a little harder and I actually have to take a step forward to keep my balance.

"I really don't want to." I shake my head and hold my breath. I know I'm being a downer, but this isn't my thing. At all.

Luckily for me, her phone rings. She instantly drops my hand to take out her phone and begins typing like a mad woman again. I use the moment to plant my ass on the barstool and take out my own cell phone. As if it would possibly have a message waiting for me.

She's texting Kevin again. I really don't see a point in being here. Hannah and Cary Ann are over on the dance floor having the time of their lives, while I'm standing by watching Eva text her boyfriend.

It goes without saying--this night totally blows.

Screw this. I pull my cell out of my clutch and click over to the messages screen. I quickly locate Ian's name.

Your shit better be gone by the time I'm back.

There it is. The same text I sent several days ago. My stomach twists into an angry knot. The message is marked as read, but Ian hasn't even bothered to reply.

No sorry. No begging for me to take him back.

He simply doesn't care.

He's probably shacked up with her right now, fucking her brains out, I tell myself. *In my bed.*

The thought enrages me and before I know it, my fingers are flying across the screen of my cell.

You're a real piece of fucking work, you know that?

I hit send before I can stop myself. Shit. I shouldn't have done that. I close my eyes, feeling pissed off at myself and at how poorly I'm handling all this shit.

I stuff my phone back in my clutch and turn to Eva. "Hey, I think I'm gonna go," I tell her over the bass of the music.

Eva looks up from her phone and sees the expression of misery on my face. She taps out something quickly and then puts her phone away. "I'll go with you," she offers. I can tell that she's worried about me now, but I don't want her to be.

"Are you sure?" I ask. "You don't have to. We just got here and it looks like Hannah and Cary Ann are having the time of their lives." I gesture toward the other end of the bar where our two coworkers are entertaining a group of young guys. One guy has his face almost resting on Hannah's chest, practically motorboating her tits.

Eva waves away my worry. "Nonsense. I can tell you're not in the mood to be here. Besides, Kevin won't quit texting me. I should go somewhere a little less busy so I can talk to him."

I start to refuse, but then I think better of it. I can tell Eva doesn't want to be here any more than I do. "Okay," I agree. "Thanks."

We go outside, where it's still bustling with tourists, and flag down a cab and within minutes are making our way back down the strip to our hotel. At the first stoplight, Eva breaks the silence and asks, "So how do you like it here? And the girls? I know they can be a little crazy, but I think you really fit in well."

"I like them, they seem pretty cool."

Eva looks at me closely, her big eyes concerned. "You're still not bothered by the cheating joke, are you?"

"No. It's cool." Yes I am. But my anger isn't for them.

Eva looks unconvinced. "You sure?"

"You know what I don't understand?" I'm forced to say.

"What?" she asks.

"How Ian couldn't even be bothered enough to tell me sorry for what he did."

"The guy's a scumbag. What would you expect from someone who was having affair with your friend?" She snorts. "If you can even call her that. I sure as hell wouldn't consider a friend to be someone that slept with my boyfriend the first chance she got."

Her words hit me in the gut. It's true. Why would I expect a selfish jerk to be repentant? "You're right," I say and nod my head. "Ian's trash. I don't know why I expect anything from him. And Sarah? She's a bitch."

"Just forget them, like yesterday's news. Let me be the first one to tell you that you're smart, beautiful, intelligent and going places. And you certainly deserve much better than a cheating asshole." She rubs my arm affectionately.

"Thank you." I bite down on the inside of my cheek before answering, "I really do like it here. Everyone's really nice."

She leans across the seat and gives me a hug as the cab slows to a stop. It's a bit awkward, but I accept it. I'm done with this. I'm done with letting Ian ruin my nights. Fuck him, and fuck Sarah.

"Come on," she says, releasing me and popping her door open. She forces it open wider with her heel and pulls me out.

A young man in a tailored black suit holds the large glass door open for us. He gives me a warm smile and I have to smile back. Inside it's so cool and calm compared to the busy and noisy streets. Our heels click on the marble floors as I walk her to the elevator, right across from the bar.

I could use a drink. That long island didn't do a damn thing and I don't want to go back to the room feeling so emotionally raw.

"You're not coming up?" Eva asks me as the elevator doors open.

I shake my head. "I want a real drink before I go pass out."

Eva bites her lower lip as she studies me. I can tell she's worried about me. Bless her heart. "Okay," she says finally, pulling me in for a brief hug. "But please don't overdo it."

She disappears into the elevator and I make my way inside the hotel's bar.

As I walk in, I remember how I left last time. I remember the gorgeous man in the suit. My body shivers as I remember the way he looked at me, the way his looks make me feel. I could really use one of those looks right now. It made me feel... sexy. Wanted.

I take the closest seat to the exit, signaling the bartender for a drink. As I wait for it, I pull out my phone and check the status of the last messages I sent Ian. They haven't been read. God. He's not even reading my texts now. I don't know why, but this makes me feel even more alone and angry.

It's not like there's anything wrong with being alone, I just didn't think I'd wind up single at this age.

I thought for sure I'd have a couple of babies with Ian by now, I think to myself sadly. I shake off the depressing thought and promise myself that I won't dwell on it anymore. As far as I'm concerned, I dodged a bullet.

The bartender comes back with my glass of cabernet. He gives me a sexy grin as he sets it down. He's a cute brunette and all, sexy even, but I'm just not feeling him. He's not my type.

My stomach twists with desire as I remember Mr. CEO again. There's just something about him. His raw sex appeal and obvious power; the way he wear his suits--like he fucking owns his dominance. It's funny, because in my life of business I'm surrounded by men in suits, but none of them look anywhere near as good as he does in them.

I smile as I bring the glass to my lips.

The bartender must think I'm smiling at him because he winks and says, "It's on the house, sweetheart," when I try to pass him a tip. He gives me a cocky smile as I watch him walk off to serve another patron. I get the feeling he's going to come back over when he's done and try to see if he'll get something for his free drink.

He'll be sorely disappointed if he does. I'm not that cheap.

I'm taking another sip of my cabernet when I suddenly feel a large hand on my waist. I nearly spit my wine out onto my blouse as thick fingers dig into my skin and I turn to push whoever it is away.

"What in the-" I turn to see a man who's gotta be in his late thirties leering at me with his bloodshot eyes. His hair's short, cut in military style and he has a serious case of dimples.

"Hey, sugar. What are you drinking tonight?" asks the man, his breath carrying the strong smell of whiskey.

My first reaction is to tell the man to get the hell away from me. But I glance around the bar and notice the upscale patrons and business people that are probably from the convention. I really don't want to cause a scene and have it get back to my boss.

"Just a glass of wine *by myself* tonight," I say politely, putting emphasis on 'by myself'.

The drunk guy fails to get the message. He tugs on his plaid tie that's already loose around his neck and wobbles as he takes the barstool next to me. Eventually, he manages to mount it and then he turns to me, practically staring at my breasts.

Okay, now I'm seriously uncomfortable.

"You've got a nice outfit on," he says in a low, gravelly voice. He leans in close, invading my personal space, so close that the smell of his breath becomes overpowering. "I think it'd look better on the floor though."

Oh hell. I need to get out of here now.

Just as I'm about to get up and leave Mr. Drunk to hump my empty barstool, I see movement out of the corner of my eye. I turn and my breath catches in my throat at the sight before me. It's Mr. CEO, walking through the bar like he owns the place, and his eyes are focused on me.

CHAPTER 7

LOGAN

I've held many business meetings at restaurants or bars just like this one. The back booth in the Madison Hotel bar is perfect for this meeting. I prefer them at times to boardrooms. It makes it easier to slip out and leave the company with a round on me. But tonight I chose this bar hoping to see my Rose again. And she didn't disappoint.

I noticed her the second she walked in. There's an air around her that commands my attention. Stevens was in the middle of a counterpoint on international resources when she walked through the open doors and walked to the same seat she was in before, directly across from the booth I chose.

I've barely listened to a word from Trent or Stevens. The

meeting's done as far as I'm concerned. We're not pushing it through until we meet agreeable terms. Stevens can insist that the cut in costs makes it worth it, but I know better. It's best not to cut corners, especially when quality and timing are concerned.

Her shapely legs are crossed and it pulls her black skirt up a little farther. She's wearing a loose slightly see-through blouse and even with the dim lighting in the room, I can easily make out her curves. Her tall heels hook onto the leg of the barstool and she sighs heavily before leaning her forearms against the bar and waiting patiently for the bartender.

She came in alone and I can't help but wonder why. My heart slows as I watch her baby blues skim the bar. She's not looking for anyone in particular. She brushes her hair out of her face and leans in slightly to order a drink. I can't hear her, not with all the other noise in this place, but her lips mesmerize me. They're a darker shade of red tonight than I've seen on her before. The deep red makes her beautiful eyes shine brighter, but that look is still there though. That sadness that's haunting her. I don't know what's causing it, but I want to find out.

"Are you going to drink that or not, Parker?" Stevens asks me from across the booth, bringing my attention back to him.

"Not," I answer and push the cold glass with the back of my hand toward Trent.

I stand tall with my shoulders squared, ready to make a

move on Rose. I may appear confident, but my nerves are getting the best of me. She could say no; she may not be interested in me in the least. Or worse, she may be taken already, though my research on her didn't turn up any partners. But I'm not going to take no for an answer.

Nothing extreme, I'm just going to offer to buy her a drink. She can't deny me such a small request. I slip off my jacket and loosen my tie.

Trent eyes me suspiciously. "Where are you headed?" he asks with a bit of suspicion in his voice. I never stay for drinks, and I never stay for anything other than business. As my right-hand man, he knows my habits.

Stevens looks past me and right at Rose. His thin lips pull into a smirk and then wider as he realizes my intentions.

"You've got a date, haven't you?" he says, raising his glass of scotch. The ice clinks as Trent leans forward and looks past me to look at Rose as well.

I stand for a moment and let a waitress pass. She gives me a heated look and blushes as she walks by. I keep my eyes straight ahead on my prize and undo the top button of my dress shirt. I don't get nervous about first impressions. I have no one to impress. My track record and bank account are enough to give me a presence in the boardroom.

"A date?" Trent asks with disbelief and then shakes his head. "She has a date, but it's not with Logan." He sits back in the booth, causing the slight shifting of the black leather seat, content with the fact that Stevens must be wrong. It's irritating that he's so sure she's not waiting for me. It shouldn't be annoyed since I shouldn't even be pursuing her, and he knows that. Still, it pisses me off. Maybe more so because she isn't waiting for me. He brings his jack and coke to his mouth as I turn to face my Rose.

And some fucker who's pawing at her.

Anger rises slowly inside me. Anger and jealousy. It's not a good look and I don't let it show, but it's there. It's heating my blood and forcing my limbs to move. His hands are on her as though she belongs to him.

My anger is relieved slightly when I take in her body language. She's not interested. She tries to push him away, but it's not happening. And that's my cue.

I leave, not bothering to look back at either of them. I know they're going to be watching; I don't give a damn what they think.

It only takes six long strides, turning my body ever so slightly between two small tables, until I'm beside her.

I lean forward, laying my jacket down and bracing my hand on the bar between my Rose and this fucker.

"I leave you alone for one night and you're already replacing me?" I look into Rose's widened eyes and wait for her to respond. Her breath hitches, and that sexual tension I've felt the last two times between us rises to a nearly unbearable level. My back is to the asshole who's still not taking the hint.

I completely ignore him.

Before she can answer me, I hear the prick clear his throat. "Hey-" His weak tone comes to a halt as I stand and turn to face him. I'm a full inch taller than him. He's got a little muscle to him and could probably get in a good hit if he wanted, but he's got nothing on me. I make it a habit to keep my body in shape. I have to. The thought makes my hands ball into fists until my knuckles turn white, but I release them just as fast.

"Yes?" I ask in a low, threatening voice, daring him to utter a response. I narrow my eyes and wait for him to make his move. He's drunk, but he's not stupid. The intimidation he's feeling is clear on his face, and he struggles to respond. He opens and closes his mouth without saying anything. His forehead's pinched and I can tell he's debating on how to handle it without looking like any more of an ass. I can feel eyes on us and the bar's noticeably quieter. We're all waiting to see what this asshole's going to do.

But he doesn't get a chance to do anything; instead, my eyes are drawn to Charlotte's small hand gripping the front of my shirt. Her other hand comes around my other side to rest just above my hip. She presses her front to my back and I stifle my groan at the feel of her breasts pressed against my lower shoulders.

I look down at her as she peeks her head around my arm to look at me. Her voice is soft but strong, and on the verge of being casual. "You wanna go?"

I look back at the asshole and he takes the chance to turn on his heel and walk off without a word. Smart move on his part. When I look back at my Rose, her eyes are on him as he leaves, and she visibly relaxes, releasing her grip on me.

I miss her touch instantly. I want it back.

As soon as I turn to face her, everything changes. A spark ignites between us and she takes a hesitant step back, suddenly realizing how close she is to me for the first time. The stool behind her scratches against the floor and her hands fall behind her to grip onto it. As though it can protect her from me.

A heated moment passes as her eyes wander down my body. I let a smirk kick up my lips and enjoy the fact that she obviously likes what she sees. The same is true on my part. Up close, she's even more beautiful. Her skin is sun-kissed, but also flushed. She has yet to disappoint me.

I wait for her eyes to find mine again. There's a blush on her cheeks, but the confident woman that took command of the stage is staring back.

"Thank you..." she says, eyeing me warily. "For that."

I hold her gaze. "No need to thank me, Rose."

"It's Charlotte-"

"Charlotte Rose... yes, I know."

"How do you know my name?" she asks suspiciously. Her breathing picks up, making her chest rise and fall a bit faster and I find my eyes drawn to her gorgeous curves. I quickly lift my gaze back to her eyes, but I know she saw.

"I saw your presentation," I answer simply and pull the stool out for her to take a seat.

"I saw." A knowing look crosses her face as she slowly sits down. She parts her lips as if to say more, but the bartender brings a drink and sets it down in front of her. He looks at me and starts to ask if I want a drink, but I wave him off.

She sees and purses her lips. There's an air of distrust around her and I can tell she's debating on getting up and walking away. But I can't let that happen.

Before she can come up with an excuse, I say teasingly, "I think you owe me at least one drink." I set my hands on the bar as I say, "I'm Logan, by the way."

"But you aren't drinking," she says, still eyeing me with caution.

"I'm not," I say easily, although the fact that it makes her suspicious pisses me off. "I'm done drinking for the night." She rests the tip of her finger on the rim of the glass as if debating if she should drink it.

"Your presentation went well," I say to change the subject. "Have you worked for that company very long?" I already know the answer, but I want to get her talking.

"I actually just started," she says a bit peppier, but her body language doesn't match the false tone in her voice. She seems angry, pissed off at me. I don't know why, but fuck, it turns me on.

"What'd you do before this?" I ask her easily before signaling the bartender. I was bred into this lifestyle, so if there's one thing my father taught me well, it's how to charm women. I haven't needed it... ever. But I know I can win her over.

"Let's see..." she pauses and straightens a little as the bartender stops in front of us.

"Could we see the dessert menu, please?" I ask. I'm going to guess she's a chocolate cake kind of woman. "You were saying?" I ask as the bartender sets down a menu and I slide it over to her. I tap on the picture of the lava cake and raise a brow.

She gives a small shake of her head. "No thanks," she says, eyeing the cake. "I don't want anything."

I grin at her refusal. I'm going to have her eating cake right out of my hand.

I wait for the bartender as she rattles off her past employer, giving me details I'd find on a resume and nothing more. When the bartender catches my eye, I hold up the menu. "The lava cake," I order and then look back at Charlotte.

"And why did you leave?" I ask with genuine curiosity. I have no idea why she left, but I'm grateful she did. Steamens Marketing never attends conferences, so I doubt I would have met her if she hadn't left.

"Because my ex is a cheating prick and my *former* best friend is a whore." The second the last word leaves her lips, she grips the stem of the glass tighter. I imagine her hands gripping my cock with the same force, and my pants grow a little tighter. "I'm sorry," she says a moment later, though it's clear she's not. I love how anger colors her voice. Makes it deeper. Sexier. "I didn't mean for it to come out like that."

My Rose has thorns.

"Nothing to be sorry about," I tell her. "I take it you worked with them?"

"Yes, that's why I left."

I nod my head and say, "So that means you're single."

She pauses for a moment, taken off guard. "I am," she says finally, her voice on edge.

"Well that's a win for me," I say as the bartender sets the cake down on the bar. Two spoons. He's a good man. Charlotte's eyeing me with a look that turns me on; half suspicion, half defiance.

"Would you like a bite?" I ask before I take a bite myself and offer her the other spoon.

She stares at the spoon for a moment. "I don't think so…"

"I insist," I say, swallowing down the cake. It's rich and velvety.

"Well, if you're going to twist my arm," she says, taking the utensil and scooping up a healthy portion. I watch as she closes her eyes and moans around the small bite of cake. My dick hardens as I picture her on her knees wrapping those lush lips around my cock.

She looks back at me with an innocent wide-eyed look. Fuck. I can't tell if she's doing it on purpose to turn me on, or if she's genuinely enjoying it.

"It's delicious," she says, wiping the bit of chocolate from the corner of her mouth and slipping her finger in quickly. "I don't usually eat dessert," she says as she takes another spoonful. "I'm always full by the time I'm done with dinner."

She continues taking small bites, savoring the cake and making my cock rock hard. All the while making casual small talk about the marketing business. She's bright and knowledgeable. My admiration for her grows, as does my sexual appetite. I have to force myself to look away and take another bite. I don't taste a damn thing though, I'm just doing it to get her to take another bite.

Each small bite seems to open her up more and more, until it's all gone and she's scraping the plate for crumbs. That forces a rough chuckle up my chest.

I lean in and whisper, my lips barely touching the shell of her ear, "You're beautiful, Rose." Her head leans back and her lips part. It takes everything in me not to take them with my own. I pull back slightly, fighting the need to restrain myself and when I do, she looks back at me with nothing but lust.

"It's Char-" she starts to respond, then stops as a chair scrapes loudly across the floor behind us.

A group of men rise and make a noisy exit. My eyes flash quickly to them and then back to my Rose who's turned to watch them leave. Her hair is on her opposite shoulder, leaving her slender neck bare. My dick twitches in my pants with the thought of leaning down and leaving an open-mouthed kiss along her neck and down to her shoulder.

"I better get going," she says suddenly. She doesn't move though.

"You don't have to; I'm enjoying your company."

"I have to be up early. The conference is early tomorrow." She looks to the doors of the bar, but again makes no move to leave. "I don't want to give my boss a reason to fire me."

"Let him. I'd hire you in an instant." I'm quick and hard with my words, and I let them resonate with her.

"I'm flattered, really. But I don't think that would be wise," she says flatly. "At all."

She's resisting. I like that. "And why's that?"

"Because... you're..." her voice trails off and she bites her lower lip. Fuck. So sexy.

"I'm what?"

Her voice is heavy when she responds. "Bad."

I chuckle. "Is that so?"

"You almost ruined my presentation, you know that?" she growls angrily, changing the subject. She's grasping at straws here. Trying to find a reason to push me away. How... cute.

So this is why she's a touch on the pissed side. "I did?" Maybe I shouldn't have made it so obvious that it pleased me when I threw her off her game.

She glares at me, only turning me on more. "Don't play coy. I lost my train of thought because of you." There's a small smile to her lips, letting me know she's not truly angry.

I grin and say, "It's not my fault that you're attracted to me."

"I think you're getting a little ahead of yourself. I said you made me lose my train of thought, not that I wanted to sleep with you." Her eyes stay fixed on the back of the bar.

My grin grows wider. "So now we're talking about sleeping with each other?"

A bright blush colors her cheeks and she doesn't respond for a moment.

I wait for her to look at me. "Tell me why," I say and stare into her eyes. She's defensive and that's fine, but she's also turned on and right now that's all I need her to be.

"Why what?" she asks without moving an inch. That guard of hers is about to crumble around her.

"Why you lost your train of thought when you saw me."

She tries to look away again, but I place my finger on her jaw and tilt her head to face me. "You did the same for me. It's only fair that I affect you just as much."

Her lips part and her eyes heat with lust at the knowledge I've given her, but she still doesn't respond. "Tell me why, my Rose."

"I don't know," she finally answers me.

"I can tell you why," I say. "You want me." She purses her lips and goes silent, clenching her thighs and licking her bottom lip. She fucking wants me. And just as much as I want her.

I lean forward. "You know what I think? I think you

would love to get to know me, that you could learn to love me being your boss."

Her breathing is coming in heavier.

"Tell me," I say and my command brings her eyes back to mine. I want to hear it directly from those beautiful lips of hers.

"I think I'd get in trouble if you were my boss," she says and her breathy words make my dick hard as fucking steel.

"Is that so?" I ask her calmly, moving my hand to her thigh and brushing my thumb back and forth against her bare skin. I lean forward and whisper into the crook of her neck, "I think I'd like that. In fact," I say and pull away to look at her face. Her head's tilted back and her eyes are half-lidded, but then she slowly tilts her head forward and looks me in the eyes. "I'd fucking love it," I conclude.

"We shouldn't do this," she whispers, but I can tell her defenses are nonexistent. She's inches away from being mine.

"We should be doing *exactly* this. I want you." I brush the pad of my thumb along her bottom lip and add, "Tonight."

Chapter 8

Charlotte

Although I'm walking with confidence behind him, I'm a ball of nerves on the inside. I shouldn't be doing this. It's reckless. Stupid, even. But my primal needs are winning the battle with common sense. I'm so messed up over Ian, I feel like I need this. I *need* Logan.

His hand splays across my back as I stand next to him at the elevator. I peek over my shoulder toward the entryway. I don't want anyone to see. This will look bad. My panic rises, but then Logan leans into me, so close I can feel his hot breath on my neck, sending shivers down my back.

"Relax," Logan says to me, his voice deep and sexy, the sound causing prickles to go up all along my arms. God, I could just melt into him. What's worse is that I can't think of a reason not to. As my eyes close with lust, the doors open with a loud *ping*, knocking me out of my trance.

He pulls me into the elevator, pressing me up against the wall.

A feeling of panic surges through me, telling me to get the hell out before the door closes. But I fight the need to run as the doors close slowly and his large body cages me in.

What's so bad about giving into my desires?

It's just one night.

A night in Vegas.

What happens here, stays here. Right?

There's nothing for me to worry about.

The thought gives me the courage to reach up and spear my fingers through his hair as he leans in for a passionate kiss and the elevator climbs the floors. I open my mouth wider and let him in, arching my body and moaning into his mouth.

His hands roam up my side, causing me to lean into him. I want him to take me. Right here, right now.

The elevator reaches his floor as I'm clawing at the buttons on his shirt. I pull away from him, breathless and nearly gasping, and he leads me down a long, ornate hallway to a large door.

He's hasty with getting the key into the door, his other hand holding mine, and when he opens it my breath catches in my throat. It's a penthouse suite, with floor-to-ceiling windows, a vast open floor plan, and stunning contemporary furniture.

Holy shit, I think to myself. *This place is incredible.* Luxury. It oozes luxury the way he oozes power.

I don't get time to admire the stunning view, because suddenly Logan is pressed against me, sending my body temperature soaring and his lips pressing hungrily against mine. His hands find my ass cheeks, gripping them tightly before lifting me into the air and my legs wrap around his waist instinctively.

He pulls away from me for a moment, keeping me perfectly balanced. Below, I can feel his big, throbbing cock pressing against my pussy, demanding entry. Fuck! God, I'm so wet for him. I suck in a heavy breath, my chest heaving with desire.

He carries me up the stairs to the loft, holding me firm every step of the way and kissing along my neck. I struggle not to squirm in his embrace as my nails dig into his crisp white dress shirt. He kicks the door shut and throws me on a king-size bed in the center of the room. I bounce on the bed with a gasp and I look up at him as he stands above me, his huge cock pressed against his slacks, my breathing a series of desperate pants.

For a moment, I'm filled with fear at what's about to take place, but burning desire sweeps it aside as Logan slowly takes off his tie and then his shirt. My legs scissor on the bed as I sit up and take in the sight of him. His muscles flex as he tosses his shirt to the floor. My pussy clenches around nothing. I push the hair off my neck, feeling hotter. I feel like I'm on fire.

It's just one night.

It feels so wrong, having a one-night stand. But I'm dying to have one with a man like him. Especially knowing he wants me as much as I want him. And no one will know. My fingers reach for the buttons on my blouse and I slowly undo them with trembling hands.

His eyes stay focused on mine. His heated gaze is a trance pinning me to the bed to do his bidding. He won't let me go.

As the silky fabric slips off my shoulders and the blouse falls into a pool around me, he makes a move to come closer for the first time. He unbuttons his pants and shoves them down as his lips attack my neck. He ravages me while he rips my bra down and sucks a nipple into his mouth.

My head falls back and soft moans spill from my lips, along with whispers and pleas for him to do what he wants to me. To take me. I don't recognize my own voice. I don't recognize the woman I am, caught in the heat of the moment and desperate for him.

My clit's thobbing as he pushes me farther up the bed and pulls my skirt down over my ass and off of me. I'm so hot for him. So wet. He groans as he cups my pussy, the thin lace the only thing separating us.

I expect him to rip them with the way he's handled me so far. But he doesn't. He sits back on his heels, and that's when I realize he's completely naked. I can barely breathe as his fingers slide gently up my thighs, leaving goosebumps and shivers up my body,

He gently pulls the lace down my ass and I have to lift up slightly for him to pull them off. His eyes stay on mine. My chest rises and falls harder with each passing second. I can't believe I'm doing this. He reaches over to the nightstand and I can't quite see what he's doing, but the sound of a wrapper makes it obvious.

Shit, I didn't even think about asking. What am I doing? As my body heats with anxiety, he pushes my legs farther apart.

I start to prop myself up on my elbows and think about backing out. It's all too fast, too soon, but his lips crash against mine and his large hand grips my hip, holding me down.

My body melds to his as he lowers his chest to mine. He nips my bottom lip as he pushes the head of his cock just slightly into my pussy. My body begs me to move, to take him in deeper, but his grip on me is relentless.

His large body cages mine in and the look in his eyes takes my breath away.

"Tell me again," he says and his deep voice vibrates up his chest. His eyes are the brightest I've ever seen as he stares at me, willing me to obey him. It takes a second for me to realize what he wants to hear.

"I want you," I say, and as the last word slips past my lips, he slams into me. His large cock fills me almost to the brink of pain. My back bows and I let out a strangled cry of pleasure. So full, so hot. He stays buried deep inside of me, letting my walls adjust to his size before pushing farther in. My legs squeeze around his hips and my toes curl. It's too much. I whimper as he pulls out slightly and then pushes forcefully back in.

He groans in the crook of my neck, "I knew you'd feel like this." I wish I could respond. I try, but nothing comes out. My neck arches, forcing my head to dig into the mattress as he fucks me at a merciless pace.

He kisses my neck as my head thrashes and he thrusts over and over into me.

My nails dig into his back as I grip onto him as though he can save me from the overwhelming sensations threatening to consume me.

His pace picks up and forces a scream from me. My body heats in intense waves as my nerve endings ignite all at once.

He rides through my orgasm, thrusting his hips at an angle that brushes against my throbbing clit each time. Pushing my orgasm higher and stronger, and dangerously close to too much.

"Logan!" I scream out his name as another release crashes through me.

My breathing is frantic at the feeling of him pushing in me to the hilt and I feel his thick cock pulsing against my tight walls.

He gently kisses my neck and my shoulder as my body

trembles beneath his.

His large frame moves away from mine, leaving the cool air to kiss my skin. He plants a single kiss against my lips and I easily return it. It's a tender touch, one I wasn't expecting.

As the highs of my orgasm come crashing down and slowly leave me in waves, I realize what I've done. I pull up the covers a little higher and wonder if I should leave.

I can hear the muted padding of his footsteps against the tiled floor as he turns on the light to the bathroom and faint light floods the room. I see my clothes on the floor. And suddenly I feel cheapened.

I knew what I was doing.

I try to calm myself as he comes back into the bedroom. His corded muscles ripple as he walks to the edge of the bed. It dips with his weight as he peels the covers back. His eyes are on my face as he does it, as though he's expecting me to protest, and a part of me wants to.

He runs a damp cloth between my legs and kisses my neck as I wince. I'm already a bit sore. I already feel regret working its way into my consciousness.

My body stiffens as he gets off the bed and leaves me with my thoughts.

I need to get out of here the moment I get the chance. And forget this ever happened.

CHAPTER 9

LOGAN

My Rose shifts in my arms. She hasn't been still since I crawled into bed next to her. Something's off. Everything was exactly how I imagined it'd be. Until it was over.

I keep my breathing steady and eyes closed. I pretend like I'm asleep. I'm not though, and I haven't been. I don't sleep well at all, let alone with someone next to me.

I know she's going to bolt. She's a runner. That's easy to tell. I don't mind, because I know she won't be running far. Come Monday, she'll be in my building and I'll have more control of the situation. Right now I'm limited.

The comforter moves slowly down my body as she slips out of the bed and lets a gentle chill in. There's a soft creak from the bed and she stills. Her breathing is the loudest sound in the room. After a moment, she finally moves. I can hear everything she does. I can practically picture her slipping her clothes into place as the sounds fill my ears.

She's sneaking out. I have to force myself not to smile at the thought. If only she knew.

I open my eyes to peek at her as I hear her walk over to my desk. What the fuck is she doing?

Everything I have is password-protected, so that doesn't matter, but if she's snooping then I have a much larger problem on my hands. Although, that could work to my benefit, but that wasn't the kind of relationship I had in mind.

My heart squeezes slightly in my chest as I hear her pick up her clutch off the nightstand. She's leaving. It's amusing in some ways, but disappointing in others. I wonder for a moment if she thinks this is what I want, or if it's her preference to leave.

I suppose it doesn't matter though. This will be the first and last time she slips out on me.

I wait a minute as I hear the door open and close with a faint click, leaving me in silence. She left. I'm not completely surprised, but it does cause a stir of emotions that I'm not fond of. There's a reason I stopped forming any attachments. People are good at leaving.

Once I'm sure she's not coming back, I move from the bed and walk straight to the desk to see what the hell she touched. A sticky note is affixed to the top of my laptop.

Sorry I slipped out, I had to go. Thank you for last night.

I huff a humorless laugh and run my finger along the feminine script. She's a runner, but I already knew that. I wasn't expecting this; it doesn't change anything though.

A wicked smile turns my lips up. She's going to be shocked on Monday. More than that, pissed.

I'm looking forward to the fight though. I know there will be one, and the thought makes my dick twitch. I look back to the empty bed and rumpled sheets. If she were here now, I'd take her again.

I'd make sure her sweet cunt was so fucking raw tomorrow she thought of me every time she sat down. It's a tight fit with her, so hopefully I left her so fucking sore it lasts until Monday.

My smile fades, and I toss the note to the desk. She's not here, and she's not mine yet.

But she will be.

I walk to the bathroom, stretching and remembering how good she felt beneath me. She was everything I wanted. I flick the light on and dig in the travel case on the counter.

It's only a matter of time before I have her again. Next time, she won't slip out in the middle of the night.

I look down at the pill case as I pop a tab open, revealing the brightly colored pills and hate it. I hate it all. I hate myself more.

I've set the pieces in play for her downfall. All because I selfishly want her.

I take three pills and swallow them, not bothering with water to wash it down.

I toss the case on the bathroom counter and walk to my briefs on the floor of the bedroom, carelessly putting them on before sitting back at the desk in the room and opening my laptop.

It's nearly 4 a.m., but there's work to do, and I know I won't be sleeping tonight. I'm sure there are at least a few dozen emails that require my immediate attention. My assistant will have a list for me in only two hours. I should finalize the other business deal I came here for, although I'm not sure I'm interested if they don't come down in price and agree to the last two terms.

I sigh heavily and run my hands through my hair. It's just another day. They'll bend to what I want, or I'll simply walk away. That's how it works in my line of business. And they know it.

As soon as the screen comes to life, her picture stares back at me. I never should have touched her. I'm a bastard for what I'm doing.

My heart clenches slightly, a feeling I'm not used to. I start to feel regret, but she loved every second of it. I made her come alive beneath me. I saw how she became paralyzed with pleasure under me. I can give her that. I can give her the escape she desperately needs.

She's running away from her past more than she's running

toward me. This will help her.

Even as I try to justify it, I know there's no good reason I should continue this. I know this is wrong. I don't give a fuck though.

I still want her. And I'm not going to take no for an answer. Nothing is going to keep me from having her.

CHAPTER 10

CHARLOTTE

I wince as I set my suitcase down in the living room of my apartment.

I'm still hurting from Logan. It's such a good hurt though. One I've never felt before.

My sore pussy clenches with desire at the thought of the previous night. The way Logan fucked me has me going through all sorts of unwanted emotions all morning. I crave the feeling of my body aching, but it was a one-time thing. Seriously, he's a master in bed--a fucking sex god. I can't help that I want more. Ian has never been that hungry for my body, nor attentive to my needs.

Selfish bastard. Neither has anyone else I've ever been with.

As I stand up straight, a feeling of guilt washes over me. I've been running from the feeling all morning, but now it's finally caught up with me.

Logan gave me the best sex of my life, I tell myself, *and I repaid him by leaving him with just a note.*

I'm not sure why I care so much. I feel horrible. Like I've committed some awful crime. Logan most likely doesn't give a shit. After all, it was just a one-night stand. And I'm sure he gets more pussy than a cat catcher. We'll never see each other again, anyway.

I set my coat down and begin unpacking when I notice a box sitting beside the couch. It's Ian's, and it's sitting exactly where it was when I left. I glare at it, anger knotting my stomach.

"I told him his shit better be gone when I got back," I mutter angrily. "Figures it's still here."

I feel like going over and kicking it, and then stomping it with all the rage I have pent up inside. I resist the urge. It won't do me any good. What I need to find out is if he's been here or not. He could just be fucking with me, trying to piss me off.

I walk into the kitchen and see that his work keys are gone. They were here when I left, so it means he came and got them, but left his box of shit.

I'm quick to grab my cell and send him a text.

You left a box of your shit here. Can you come get it, please?

I want to add on 'asshole' at the end of the message, but I exercise immense restraint and just press send. I stare at the screen and wait for a response before adding:

If you don't come get it, I'm going to donate it to the Salvation Army.

He's had plenty of time, and I've been more than reasonable. I wait for a reply, but after it becomes clear he's not going to respond, I let out a sigh and set my cell on the table. Staring at it and resisting the urge to smash it with a hammer, just because it reminds me of him.

"I need a cup of coffee," I mutter, walking over to the Keurig machine, starting it, and then sitting down in a kitchen chair. I bought this dining set right before he moved in. My first meal at this table was with him. I cooked something special, I don't remember what. I let out a long exhale and try to ignore the painful reminder that I once loved him. I gave him everything I had.

Sighing, I place my head in my hands and try to calm my racing thoughts.

I focus on work. That's always a good outlet. It's productive and motivating. But even after acing my presentation at the convention, I feel stressed. There's a meeting on Monday and I have to be prepared, but with thoughts of Logan and the prospect of dealing with Ian on my mind, it's going to be a struggle.

I'm on edge and afraid of losing my job. I was hired as a temp, so I'm essentially on a probationary period. All signs point to me being just fine, but I'm feeling so damn insecure. Even though after how good I did with my presentation, I should be more than fine. I guess I'm worried because after losing Ian, my job is the only thing I have left.

At this point, I need my job just to stay sane, I tell myself as I pick at the loose thread on the tablecloth. I need a new one. I need a new everything.

Definitely a new man... like Logan. I wish I were back in Logan's bed, being devoured, feeling wanted. No man has ever made me feel like that before. I felt... powerful sleeping with a man of his stature.

I shake off the desire and the guilt from leaving.

It's best that I left the way I did and nipped that in the bud. A relationship between us would've ended badly anyway. I could easily see myself getting attached to him and then being discarded like yesterday's news. I don't need a man right now. I run my hands down my face and get up as I hear the coffee machine spurting out the last few drops.

I don't need anyone. I pour a ton of sugar in my mug and then stir it up before sitting back down.

Monday morning will be here before I know it. Then I can stop all this worrying and just focus on work.

I take a nice, relaxing sip of coffee and already feel a little better, so I check my phone. Still no message from the asshole even though it's marked as read. Fucking hell. I slam it down on the table and grip my coffee cup.

"Whatever," I mutter, resisting the urge to send him a particularly nasty text. I am a better person than this, and I do not need to lower myself to his level.

I get up from the table and walk into the living room and take my anger out on Ian's box instead, delivering several sharp kicks to it. My coffee's in my hand and the first kick sends a little spilling over the side of the box. I don't care. I use the inside of my foot so it doesn't hurt. Or maybe I'm just not kicking hard enough since there's only a small pathetic dent in the side of the cardboard. Whatever. I feel better. Sort of.

Not nearly as good as I felt last night.

If being with Logan taught me anything, it's that Ian didn't know a goddamn thing about putting it down in the bedroom. Just thinking about it causes my pussy to throb with need and pain, a reminder of how hard Logan fucked me. Shivers tingle down my spine and send goosebumps over my body.

Shit, I need to go upstairs and work until I pass out and get him out of my head. It's the best thing for me.

Pushing Logan from my mind, I check all the messages on my landline and make sure the doors are locked before turning in for a long night of work. As I climb the stairs to my room, I realize getting Logan, his powerful body, and his massive cock out of my mind will not be an easy task.

It's definitely going to be a long weekend till Monday.

CHAPTER 11

CHARLOTTE

Thank fuck it's Monday. Getting Logan off my mind... well, it didn't happen. I got a ton of work done and even forgot about my asshole ex. But every time I fell asleep, I dreamed of Logan's touch. That's not a good sign. And waking up horny and lonely is not a good combination.

As I climb out of the car and head to the building, I know I need to immerse myself in work and forget about both Ian and Logan.

I walk into the office building, shoving the door open with my forearm as I carry my daily morning coffee in one hand, and a paper bag with a tempting donut I couldn't resist in the other, and do a double take.

What the fuck? I think in panic. There are boxes everywhere. Literally, everything in the front room is packed away. Feeling weak in the knees, I lean against the doorjamb, my breathing coming in shallow gasps, my heart pounding.

Oh my God! I yell in my mind. *The company sold out.* There were rumors last week of a buyout, but I thought they were just rumors. Fuck!

As I try to calm my racing heart, I think of every other place close by that I can apply to. I need a job as soon as fucking possible. But there's literally nowhere else. I know. I just fucking applied everywhere two weeks ago!

"Are you okay?" asks a familiar voice near my ear.

I jump and let out a little cry of surprise as I drop the bag with my donut. "Jesus, Eva!" I complain, turning to face her with my hand over my heart.

She looks beautiful today in her black pantsuit and dark glossy heels, her hair pulled back in a businesslike ponytail. More than that, she looks fine. Calm, even. "You scared the shit out of me," I say admonishingly. I gesture nervously at all the boxes. "What the fuck is going on?" I ask in a hushed voice as I bend to pick up my bag.

Eva looks at me with apprehension and then lets out a laugh. "Someone's bought the company. But don't worry, it's a silent partnership." She sounds all peppy and happy. I don't know if she's got inside information that's making her feel secure, or if she's just naive. "We have a board meeting about

it in like five minutes." She leans in close and whispers, "You didn't read your email on Friday, did you?"

"Shit." I just breathe the word. I don't remember an email, but my head has been so lost in thought.

Eva shakes her head. "It's fine," she says as she waves it off and walks with me to the meeting room in the back corner of the building. "From what I can gather, the company was forbidden to talk about the sale while it was under contract. That's why I'm guessing we never heard about it." She places a comforting hand on my shoulder, seeing the worry etched across my face. "Don't worry, Charlotte. We've been assured that our jobs aren't in any danger."

"How can we trust that?" I ask. "You know how those corporate heads at the top think. They don't give a crap what happens to us down at the bottom." Anxiety is coursing in my blood. I wish I could trust her, but I can't.

"Because it's under the terms and conditions in the agreement of the sale. They can't fire any current employees for several years."

"Are you absolutely sure?"

"Positive."

I let out a small sigh of relief I relax slightly, bringing my coffee to my lips. I make a promise to myself not to freak out until I have a real reason to.

"But there's a catch," Eva adds, and I hold back a groan. "Part of the agreement involves relocating, hence all the boxes."

Behind Eva, I watch as several people walk into the boardroom. I can handle this change. Sometimes change is good.

I shift the bag to hold it in one hand along with my coffee so I can scratch at the back of my neck as we walk into the room and take our seats. "Where's the new building?" I ask her quietly. Everyone around us is engaged in quiet small talk, too.

"Parker-Moore on the city skyline," Eva replies. "About a half hour from here?"

I nod, but I'm not really happy. "That sucks." I vaguely recognize the company name. I almost applied for a job with them, but I didn't. The skyline is a far drive. This place is nearly a half an hour-long commute for me. So now I'm looking at an hour-long drive, and that's without traffic.

"Yeah, it does." Eva nods in agreement. "But it could be worse. We could all be looking at pink slips right now and a shitty severance that barely covers a month's worth of living expenses."

I sigh. "I guess you're right."

Mr. Hastings walks into the room, waving his hands to quiet the room of gossiping employees. "I know some of you are concerned with the buyout, but please rest assured that none of your jobs are in jeopardy. I'll kindly ask you all to go with the flow for now, as this is just another normal day working here, and help with packing things up."

"For those of you who have long commutes to get here

already, temporary housing will be available for you if you need it. If you don't want, or are unable to move your items yourself, please label them and move them against the far wall."

Hannah stands next to Hastings with a stack of large booklets in her hand. Mr. Hastings gives her a tight smile and then gestures at the bundle she's holding. "Hannah here has all the packets of information you'll need about the new company and housing. All of you are expected to have moved and completed the transfer by the end of the workday, and will be required to attend the group board meeting tomorrow."

I barely pay attention to the questions everyone asks and the vague answers Hastings has

as I accept my packet of information from Hannah, and try to stop worrying about the long drive that I'm going to have now. At least I have a job. I keep telling myself that throughout the meeting. That's what matters.

The meeting's finally adjourned, and I return to my office without a word. There are moving supplies lined up against the far wall and I grab a roll of packing tape and a few boxes. I think I'll only need two.

Eva's gabbing with the other girls, but I just want to get this going and begin sifting through my things, making sure everything's in order. I can talk to them later, when I'm calm and less on edge. My hands tremble as I organize my things, a feeling of anxiety overtaking my body.

I hate this shit. I don't want to have to relocate. I tape

up the bottom of one box and cringe at the sound of the tape pulling from the roll. I grit my teeth as I pick up the things from my desk and easily set everything in the box. It's like deja vu. I just did this. I close my eyes and cringe. I just fucking did this.

Eva comes in when I'm almost finished taping up the last of my boxes and I try to keep a positive vibe around me. I don't want my negativity rubbing off on her.

"You know, this could turn out to be pretty good," she tells me as she steps into my small office. It's really small and with her in the doorway, it already feels cramped.

She has a stack of papers in her hand and a smile on her face. "I heard we're going to be getting raises, and the new company is going to be bringing in an influx of clients." She leans against the wall, making herself comfortable. "Hastings is so excited about this. He told me there's going to be *huge* opportunities for us."

"I'll believe it when it happens," I say skeptically.

"Pessimist," Eva teases. She begins to walk out of the room, but then stops. "Hey, you know what? I just looked up our new boss on my phone. He's fucking crazy hot. Like seriously, I don't even know how he's a CEO of company and not out modeling somewhere."

Probably not as hot as Logan, I think to myself.

"Let me see," I say. I almost want to tell her about Logan... I wanna brag, but I shouldn't. A one-night stand doesn't color

anyone in a pretty light.

"You're gonna totally flip," Eva warns me. She walks over to my desk and sets her papers down and then pulls her cell out the pocket of her chic-as-fuck pantsuit. I eye it with a hint of jealousy as she brings up the picture. "Say hello to our new boss. Or as I'd like to say, BILF." She takes out her phone and brandishes it my face, grinning with absolutely glee. "See? Isn't he the hottest fucking thing you've ever seen?"

My heart nearly stops at the grinning face staring back at me. Eva stares at me, waiting for me to react, but I can't speak. Not a single. Fucking. Word.

Oh my God. It's him.

CHAPTER 12

LOGAN

I lean back on the bench. It's nearly six thirty and I need to leave. I'm anxious to leave, in fact. I haven't been this damn excited for work in years.

The crisp morning air whips across my freshly shaven face. It feels refreshing as I take a deep inhale and listen to the wind. The soft, relaxing sounds are interrupted by my father's low, gruff voice. Bringing me back to the present.

"How was the conference?" he asks me. His voice is a bit muffled. It's not the strong tone I grew up with. His stroke left him paralyzed down his entire left side.

I lean forward with my elbows on my knees and look up at him. He's on the opposite bench. I'm facing the the stone wall of the back of the nursing home and he's overlooking the woods behind me. "Productive. I knew it would be."

His nods his head and looks behind me. The daylight is just rising through the trees behind the nursing home. It's private and the gardens are comforting for my father. Or so he says.

"So you settled on which of the two?" he asks. Although the stroke left him physically impaired, he's mentally the same man he's always been, and I do my best to include him. Although I don't have to. But it gives him something to do that's useful. His life used to revolve around work. It was all he had. Growing up, I barely ever saw him and when I did, he made sure I knew I was being groomed to take over the business.

We didn't have father-son time. We had business training. At times I resented him. I hated watching my mother lose interest in the two of us. She looked at me as though it was my fault that he spent every waking moment in his office. I don't remember a time that she looked at me with love. She hated that I was just like him. Even though I had no choice, that didn't matter to her.

"Armcorp."

His brow furrows and he pats his right hand against his leg. I can tell he's not happy with the decision.

"Fairmont would have been better," he says simply. He hasn't been happy with many of my decisions over the last seven years. Each year I've branched further and further away from his counsel.

"I wanted this one." I tell him the truth, which is more than I gave Trent. I won't admit to anyone that I made a business decision because of a woman.

His eyes flash to mine. "Wanted?"

"Yes," I say simply. I wanted it, so I took it. I wanted *her*. There's no discussion on this matter. I'm the CEO, this was my decision, and as selfish as it was, it's done. I'm not turning back on my word.

My father must sense how I've come to terms with this choice. He doesn't push me for more. As I stare back at him and his eyes move to the forest behind me, I see him for who he is in this moment. Once a strong man of power, now weak and reliant on others. I grit my teeth, hating that this is the way it works. I'll be him one day. In many ways, I already am.

"How are the treatments going?" he asks after a long quiet moment.

"Everything's fine." I look him in the eyes as I answer.

He breaks eye contact and the corners of lips turn down into a scornful frown. "That's what your mother used to say."

I don't hide my scowl. I hate it when he brings her up. I hate thinking about her in general. My father may have raised me to be a cold, ruthless fuck incapable of real attachments and emotion, but at least he tried to be there for me.

My mother is a money hungry bitch. She took my father for everything he had and moved on to the next rich man she could spread her legs for. I was a hindrance for her. I haven't spoken to her in at least three years, maybe more. I don't need this today.

I give my father a tight smile. "I need to get going."

He eyes me, but nods slightly.

"Come back tomorrow," he says without looking at me.

I don't know why I even come here anymore. Some false sense of obligation to a man who never knew me, I guess. He gave me this life. He raised me to be the man I am. I should be grateful. Men would kill to be in my position, but I want something more. I don't want to end up like him.

I nod, unsure of whether or not he sees and walk quickly through the path at the front of the nursing home. My Aston Martin's out front, waiting for me. I usually have Andrew drive me so I can get work done in the limo during the drive. But not today. Today is different.

I try to remember the easy feeling I had this morning. The excitement of seeing her reaction as I settle into my seat and look at the phone sitting on top of my suit jacket. I'll be in the office in twenty minutes, but I want to know now if she's already there.

Charlotte. I did this for her. She could quit though. I imagine the thought has crossed her mind more than once since she found out.

As I go through the list of signatures, I spot her feminine writing.

I lean back easily as I start my car. It rumbles with a soft purr of satisfaction that mirrors what I'm feeling.

At least I have my Rose waiting for me.

CHAPTER 13

CHARLOTTE

"Can you believe how amazing this is?" I ask Eva, staring up at the tall Parker-Moore skyscraper. We're both preparing to go inside for our first day of work, starting with the board meeting, but have to stop to admire the workmanship of Parker-Moore. This building has to be the tallest and finest corporate building in all of downtown.

Eva shades her eyes, squinting up into the sky. "It sure beats Armcorp's, that's for sure. Makes it look like a hut."

"I guess we're about to get a pay raise," I predict, stifling a yawn that creeps up regardless of the fact I'm an emotional wreck. Last night I was unable to sleep because my thoughts were consumed by Logan and what this all meant. I feel awful that I'm this exhausted on my first day at my new job, and I'm almost convinced I'm going to mess something major up and end up out on the street. At least Eva's company during our carpool kept my mind off of Logan. And the fact that he's now my boss. Thinking about it causes anxiety to wash through me, but I shove it down, gripping my purse as if it can save me. "There's no way we won't," I say with as much confidence as I can manage.

Eva tears her eyes away from the tall building and growls, "You're damn right we will."

Our heels click across the polished marble floors as we enter the lobby, and my jaw nearly drops. It's even more beautiful on the inside than it is the outside. The walls are painted a muted shade of taupe, and they're adorned with gorgeous antique paintings that must've cost a fuckton. Complementing everything is upscale, contemporary furniture. Seriously, some of this stuff I wish I could steal and take home to put in my living room.

On top of that, in the middle of the room sits a beautiful marble fountain with a naked Greek statue at its center, filling the giant lobby with the soothing sounds of running water. Meanwhile, classical music plays softly over a speaker system giving the atmospheric vibe a very relaxing feel.

It feels so high class in here.

"I feel like a high-class whore now," Eva whispers to me as we watch employees making their way to whatever departments they're headed to.

"I know, right?" I say, swallowing back another yawn.

We share a nervous smile and then continue on to the hallway and enter an elevator. Thankfully, no one else gets on, and it's just the two of us. Eva presses the button for the top floor, and the door slides close.

As we rise to the top floor, I start feeling even sicker with anxiety. This is a big day for me, and I don't want to fuck it up somehow. I keep feeling like something bad is going to happen and I'm going to end up without a job, even though I should be confident in my abilities. It's because of Logan. I have no clue what he's going to say or do when I see him.

By the time we reach the top floor, I feel like I'm going to hurl.

Seeing my worry, Eva gives me a pat on the back before we leave the elevator. "It's gonna be okay," she assures me. She has no fucking clue.

I'm a ball of nerves as we enter the new boardroom. I literally feel like I'm trembling all over. For a moment, I want to run away and flee the building.

You have to stop this, I tell myself, steeling my resolve. *You are in control. There is nothing you can't do.*

As we make our way to two empty seats around the large mahogany meeting table, my heart skips a beat.

Logan's sitting at the head of the table, looking sharp as a tack in his grey, crisp business suit, his hair gelled and slicked to the side. God, he's so fucking handsome. He looks like he owns the entire room, like corporate royalty. I can feel his eyes on me, boring into me with an intensity that causes my skin to prickle.

I'm forced to look away, my cheeks burning, my mind filled with images of our night of hot sex.

I don't know how I'm going to get through this, I think as I lower myself in my seat and place my briefcase on the table, doing my best to avoid his gaze. Honestly, I feel like Logan can make me cum by just looking at me. Lord knows how fucking horny I am, having thought about his hot body and massive cock all night. I couldn't help it. I almost didn't come. But I need this job. If I didn't, I would have quit the second I found out he was my new boss.

Unconsciously I bring my thighs close together and my pussy clenches with need. Shit, my panties are wet. I'm annoyed by this, but I can't help it. I'm practically burning up with a desire that's almost painful.

In fact, if I were a guy, I'd have a case of blue balls right about now. The funny thought does nothing to ease the tension running through my body.

Noticing my obvious discomfort, Eva glances over at me. "You alright?" she asks softly.

"Yeah," I say, my voice strained. "Just a little nervous."

She smirks and nods toward Logan while leaning in and whispering, "He's absolutely gorgeous, isn't he?"

You have no fucking idea.

"Fucking fabulous," I mutter, keeping my eyes carefully in the safe zone.

Luckily for me, the meeting officially begins and several speakers get up to talk about the merger, going over the finer details of the contract. A lot of it was already told to us by Hastings and is outlined in the pamphlets we received the day prior.

I concentrate on keeping my eyes on the speakers, until the last one sits.

Logan rises to his feet and speaks for the first time. His rough baritone voice sends shivers through my body. He stands tall and commanding. It's obvious that he's the one in charge, and he should be.

I try to ignore the effect he has on me and when that doesn't work, I try to ignore him entirely, concentrating on the table, the blank projection screen behind him. The beautiful wallpaper in the room. Anything and everything except for him.

He begins announcing job positions of his new employees. I listen intently, half marveling at how sexy and deep his voice sounds, and half wanting to get up and run from the room. I don't expect Logan's going to call my name for anything important, and if he does, I'm convinced he's going to regulate me to an intern position just to put me in my place for slighting him. The thought makes my stomach twist with anxiety. I fucking hope not. I don't know if I'll be able to handle myself if he does. Thoughts of trying not to call him out and making a fool of myself run rampant in my mind.

When he says my name, however, I almost need to be picked up off the floor.

"Miss Harrison is the new head of the sales department," Logan announces, turning to look at me with a mischievous smile, his eyes sparkling with mirth.

Almost immediately, Eva gives me a congratulatory pat on the back followed by a thumb up, her eyes sparkling with pride. "Congrats, girl!" she whispers fiercely. "You deserve it." I feel all eyes in the room on me and several of my coworkers start whispering amongst themselves.

Meanwhile, I'm unable to react, frozen with disbelief. Seriously, I'm fucking floored and feel absolutely sick to my stomach. I mean, what is Logan thinking? After the night we shared, this has to be a huge fucking conflict of interest.

And it's the reason why he did it, I say to myself, noticing the way Logan is getting a kick out of this. He did this on purpose. I wonder how long he'll play up this charade. I've never had a position like this before. Head of Sales. I don't know if I can handle it.

Maybe that's why he assigned it to me. I don't know what to think. I don't know how I should feel either. I don't know if I should be angry, but I damn sure am shocked.

Looking like he's firm and confident in his decision, Logan outlines my role and duties in great detail. I'm to be in charge of twelve new clients, all of whom are from his company and have no marketing strategy, and we launch in four weeks.

"You can create your own team," Logan says when he's finished outlining what I need to do, "but you will be solely responsible for each of the launches."

I sit there, simmering with disbelief and worry. Being new, I have practically no resources at my disposal to make things happen so quickly.

"Mr. Parker," Hastings politely interrupts. He's sitting near the head of the table, next to Logan's seat. "I think you're asking a bit much of Charlotte. She's new here." Nausea threatens to humiliate me. Even my boss who had all the praise in the world for me doesn't think I can handle it.

Logan turns to survey Hastings with a grim expression. "There's a reason Armcorp hired her and then made her the keynote speaker. I was there for the presentation. And I plan to take full advantage of Miss Harrison."

CHAPTER 14

LOGAN

"Miss Harrison?" I raise my voice so Rose can hear me as everyone starts filing out of the room. She was the first to stand when the meeting was concluded, and it's obvious she's making a run for it. She wants to get away from me, but I'm not done with her yet.

She turns slowly to face me, pulling at the sleeve of her blouse as she says, "Yes, Mr. Parker?" Hearing her soft, sweet voice makes me want her even more. It was difficult enough to restrain myself throughout the hour-long meeting. Now that it's over, I'm ready to face my Rose. I'm anxious to see her reaction. She's obviously affected, but the lack of an outward reaction has me on edge.

"Stay for a moment, please. I'd like to have a word."

Trent speaks in a low voice as he stands to leave, "Let's meet at three to go over these last two files."

I nod although I'm not quite paying attention. It can wait.

A woman next to Charlotte, obviously a friend, asks quietly if she wants her to stay behind. I narrow my eyes and wait for her to respond. I can barely hear her over the sounds of everyone else leaving and quietly talking to one another. I don't hear what Charlotte says, but I see her shake her head no. It soothes the beast inside of me pacing with the need to be alone with Rose. Good girl. She may have conflicting feelings, but she's playing along for now.

I can feel Hastings looking back at me as he exits, waiting to catch my eye, but I ignore him and gesture to the chair in front of me while making eye contact with Rose instead. I wait a moment, watching her hesitantly stand at her chair while the rest of the company files out around her.

"I'd like to talk to you afterward, Charlotte," Hastings says to her loud enough for me to hear. I resist the urge to smirk at him. He can feel however he wants about her being head of sales. They picked her to do that presentation for a reason. She's damn good at what she does. We need to impress clients, and she knows how to do that. I don't give a fuck if it's a lot of pressure on her, she'll learn to adjust.

It's a new department, and I can appoint whoever the hell I want to that position. And I'm choosing her. Whether he likes it or not.

Charlotte makes her way over to me and takes a seat, putting her hands in her lap and looking everywhere but at me. She's nervous. I fucking love it. I love that I'm getting to her.

Everyone files out and as Trent exits, I call out to him, "Please close the door behind you, Trent." He's the last one to leave.

His eyes dart from me to Charlotte with a slight unspoken question, but he doesn't object.

The door closes with a loud click, leaving us alone.

I'm sure the only thing on her mind is our night together and the way she left me.

I imagine she's rethinking that decision to sneak out and leave me with only a sticky note. If she thought she could get away that easily, she knows better now.

I shift forward in my seat so I can take off my suit jacket and ask her, "I need to know when you'll have a sales pitch ready."

She blinks a few times with her lips parted in shock.

I resist the urge to show her how much I'm enjoying this and instead set my jacket gently on the table. I rest my elbow on the table and place my head in my hand, looking at her beautiful blue eyes and waiting for a response.

After a moment she clears her throat. "I'll need a few days to go through all of the products and the ideal placements." Her voice is strained, and she shifts uncomfortably in her seat.

She hesitantly parts those lush lips and I know she wants

to ask about that night, but she doesn't. Her cheeks burn a bright red as I stare at her with a blank face waiting for more. Her breathing picks up a bit and she refuses to look me in the eyes. A sadness crosses her face that has me questioning this game I'm playing. Maybe she thinks I don't remember.

There's no way that I could ever forget that night. But she doesn't know that.

"Sorry," she says and pulls at the hem of her skirt, not looking at me, "I'm just a little…"

She breathes in deep.

I sit upright and lean forward, close enough to touch her, but I don't. "A little what, Rose?" A knowing look flashes in her eyes at my pet name for her. I arch a brow and wait, but she just stares at me like a deer in headlights.

"I asked you a question; when will you have the sales pitch?"

She clears her throat and squares her shoulders, seeming to right herself. All trace of emotion gone, now that she knows what I'm doing.

"I'll need at least this workweek. I can have something to you by Monday for the first one, but nothing will be finalized until I can arrange meetings with our business partners." For the first time today, a smile grows on my face.

"You presentation skills are excellent." I look past her, remembering her presentation at the conference. She's amazing at what she does. And she's youthful, and a beautiful woman at that. It's going to be hard for them to tell her no.

"You were meant to lead the sales department. Don't let anyone tell you differently."

A small, sweet smile plays at her lips although it doesn't get rid of the apprehension in her expression. "Thank you, Mr. Parker," she answers respectfully and looks to the door.

"Thank you, Miss Harrison, that's all."

She looks flushed and parts her lips, but doesn't say anything.

"Are you alright?" I ask her.

She gives me a smile and nods, holding the folders she came in with close to her chest.

"I'm fine, thank you." Her response is short and expected.

"I'll see you on Friday at the next meeting." She purses her lips and looks at the door and then back at me. My heart pounds in my chest. I can tell she's debating on saying something. She doesn't though. She opens her mouth once, but slams it shut and stands up, smoothing her skirt quickly and then takes a single step to move around me.

I make my move then. My hand reaches out and brushes against her thigh, skimming up her skirt slightly.

She gasps slightly and wavers on her heels.

"One more thing," I say as I turn her to face me, putting my other hand on the back of her knee.

"The note you left... I'm choosing to ignore it." Her breath hitches, and her sweet lips part for a moment before she moves out of my grasp and takes a step back.

"I don't think we should do this," she says slowly, her eyes staying trained on mine. She sounds unsure, because she is.

"I think we should," I say as I stand in front of her.

Her breathing comes in heavy pants. I stand and take a step toward her as she takes a step small back. "I still want you."

I splay my hand on her back and walk her to the door, but I don't open it. She moves to leave, but I put my hand on the door and stand behind her.

"I thought it was over in Vegas," she says softly. She looks at the door and then at me. "I can't-"

"You can." I cut her off. "This is just me and you."

Her eyes search my face as I speak. "There's work, and then there's this." I lean in and plant a soft kiss on her lips. Hers are hard at first, but they quickly mold to mine. Yes! My hardened dick strains against my zipper. I should take her against the wall right now. But I can't. Not yet. She's hesitant, and I can't push just yet.

I kiss her deeply and with a passion that echoes what we had that night together. Her back arches slowly and her hands slowly slip up my shirt, letting her fingers trail along my hard chest.

I pull her hips toward me so she can feel how hard I am for her. I want her, and I need her to know that. She lets out a small moan. I lean forward, breaking our kiss and whisper in the crook of her neck, "My sweet Rose, it's not over until I say it's over."

CHAPTER 15

CHARLOTTE

"**I**'m worried about you, Charlotte," Hastings tells me in a hushed voice. He takes off his reading glasses and sets them on his desk, looking at me as though he feels sorry for me.

I knew this was coming when I walked in here this morning. He was too busy to meet with me yesterday by the time I left the *meeting* with Logan. So now I'm sitting in his office trying hard not to be offended, while also trying to project the confidence that I can do this. "I think that Logan is doing you a disservice, putting that much on your plate so soon."

"I'll be okay," I say confidently, flashing an easy smile. Though I'm trying to seem upbeat, I'm not at all. If the shock and self-consciousness about all this shit with the buyout and Logan weren't enough, I got into a nasty fight with Ian last night. He showed up without warning on my doorstep, demanding that I let him in.

I told him that he no longer lived with me, but he wasn't taking no for an answer. He tried to push his way in, but I slammed the door in his face. He has a key, which sucks. But I had a bolt. So he was fucked. Last night, anyway, since today's a different story and in the pit of my stomach I know this is going to be an issue. I called the landlord and asked him to change the locks. I'm just praying they get it done in time before that asshole locks me out.

I spent the rest of the night laying in bed, hating Ian and this shit position I'm in. The only other thing I could concentrate on was how Logan wanted me yesterday. All I could do was think about how hot Logan looked in the boardroom, how sexy he made me feel I was shocked at the sudden turn of events with him taking over the company and naming me head sales rep, but I'm convinced he's up to something.

He's the cat, and I'm the mouse.

I don't care what Logan's plans are, I think to myself angrily. *I'll show him that I'm not some toy to be played with on a whim.* Yesterday I was caught off guard and shocked. Today's a new day.

Thinking about the way Logan looked at me yesterday in the boardroom causes my blood to heat with desire. It pisses me off that I'm turned on by a man who's toying with me. What's worse is that my job is at stake. My heart clenches, but rather than be worried and upset, I hold onto the anger. Without realizing it, I find myself scowling at Hastings in irritation.

Hastings frowns at me, his bushy eyebrows drawing together. "You're glaring at me, Charlotte, did I offend you?"

"Oh, no, Mr. Hastings," I say, quickly morphing my scowl into a smile. "I'm just thinking about how I'm going to go about preparing for a successful launch with the resources I have at my disposal."

Goddamnit, Logan.

Before Hastings can respond, there's a knock at the door. I turn to see Eva poking her head in the doorway. She looks the consummate professional today with her hair in an elegant French twist and dressed in a crisp white pantsuit that makes me want to go shopping. "Good morning, Mr. Hastings. You're looking mighty handsome today."

Mr. Hastings chuckles, his cheeks turning a rosy red, and waves his hand dismissively. "Oh stop it, Eva. How are you enjoying the merger?"

"It's going better than I expected," Eva replies, giving me a smile. "It doesn't hurt when you have such an awesome boss to help smooth things out with the new one." She bats her eyelashes, and Mr. Hastings turns redder.

I shake my head. Eva must want something from Hastings, and knowing her, she's most likely going to get it.

The two talk about business matters for a moment. Specifically, the new building, commuting, and Hastings gives her a bullet list of things to do to get everything up and running smoothly. Meanwhile, all I can think about is how I'm going to handle Logan. I have no fucking clue. As I come to that conclusion, Eva turns her gaze on me. "Ready for lunch?"

"What's on your mind, girlie?" Eva asks as she dips a salty french fry in a pile of ketchup. "I can tell something's been bothering you."

For lunch, we've settled on an upscale cafe down the street from our new workplace. We're seated in the middle of the cafe in a small two-person booth. Between the two of us we're enjoying two big burgers, fries, a vanilla shake and a diet Coke. It's a pretty swanky restaurant, with gleaming marble floors, gold-plated trim and crown molding. I love the burgundy and white color scheme, and the ambience is relaxed.

Too bad I'm a swirling canopy of emotions and can't calm down and enjoy it.

Should I tell her? I wonder. *And would she even believe me?*

I grip onto my diet Coke with both hands, debating inwardly. It could look very bad if I told Eva that I slept with Logan in a moment of weakness. I like to think that she'd understand, but I'm not sure I want to risk it.

Don't, I decide finally. *No matter how much I trust her, there's no telling what could happen if word got out that I slept with the boss.*

When it comes down to it, I don't want Eva to think less of me. She's been a good friend, my only friend really, and I would hate to lose her at a time where I'm going through so much in my life.

"Nothing," I say with a sigh, "it's just this merger is proving to be stressful. The extra commute time, being handed all this responsibility right off the bat. And my breakup with Ian."

Eva frowns at me and washes down her fry with a slurp of her vanilla milkshake. "I'm sorry, Charlotte. I don't know why Logan is putting so much pressure on you." She pauses to dip another fry in ketchup. "Did Ian come get his stuff?"

I nod and then scowl at my untouched burger. I'm such a bundle of nerves that I can't even think about eating. "Ummm," I say, "we kind of got into a fight."

"Kind of?" Eva sits back against the booth. "You're broken up; what's there to fight about?"

"Yeah. He wanted back in, but I wouldn't let him. I mean, can you believe this guy? He thinks he should be able to stay in our apartment after what he did? I ended up throwing all his stuff outside. We started yelling at each other, cursing each other out. Girl, it was awful."

"Well, at least you got to tell that douche how you really felt."

"That's the thing. I'm mad that I did it. It didn't change anything. He's not going to say sorry or beg me to take him back. All it did was show how much I still cared."

Just thinking about the previous night makes me angrier. I still can't believe Ian hasn't had the decency to tell me sorry or begged for my forgiveness. After he got caught cheating, his personality took a 180 degree turn. Like Dr. Jekyll and Mr. Hyde, I'd been sleeping with a stranger the whole time I was with him. And to think that he should be allowed to sleep under the same roof with me after what he did? The nerve of that prick!

Eva reaches across the table and puts a hand on my arm concernedly. "Charlotte, don't be so hard on yourself. You're only human. It's only natural to have those emotions."

I sniffle, staring at my burger. "You're right, Eva. I need to stop thinking about it. I wish he'd just move the fuck out so I can let him go live his happily ever after with Sarah."

I give them two months, I think to myself, *before they're at each other throats and Ian is cheating on her with a new whore.* The nasty thought only makes me want to cry. What if it was really me, and not him? What if they do get their happily ever after? I shove down the thought and stuff another fry into my mouth before I cry any more over that asshole.

Eva smiles at me and takes a sip of her vanilla shake. "That's the spirit. Fuck Ian! You'll find your own happily ever after with some sex god that's better in bed than Ian. You'll see."

I almost choke on how ironic her words are, though I think a fairytale ending with Logan has zero chance of happening. "I wish."

Eva sets down her shake and fans herself with both hands. "Oh, oh! Speaking of happily ever afters and sex gods, did you see how hot Logan looked in the boardroom yesterday? My God, that man is pure sex on legs!"

"He's alright," I lie, trying to keep my thoughts G-rated. Eva needs to stop bringing up how hot Logan is, especially when it's hard enough to get the man out of my mind. "Nothing you can't see in any GQ magazine."

Eva gives me a look. "What? You're crazy. On a scale of one to ten, that man is a hundred! Shit, if I weren't in a relationship with Kevin..." Eva makes a sound and shakes her head.

I don't know how I feel with Eva going crazy over Logan. On one hand, she's in a happy relationship and I know that she's just joking around, but on the other, I want to tell her about my predicament so she'll stop bringing him up. I know it's not like he's mine or anything, but I don't like her talking about him like that.

When I don't reply right away, Eva frowns. "Look, if you're so worried about commuting, why don't you sign up for the temporary housing the company's offered? It'll help until you can find a place nearby to move to."

I pick up a fry and take a small bite. It's extra salty, like how I feel inside. After a few halfhearted nibbles, I put it down. It's all my stomach can handle right now. "I thought about it, but I don't know," I say. If I take the housing offer it'll only be one more thing that Logan has over me, and I don't know if I can abide by that.

Eva takes another sip of her shake, this time nearly draining it to the bottom. "Well you better decide before you end up knee-deep in work and don't have time to get it done. You can't fail your startup because you're overworked and tired from working long hours and then having to commute long distances."

I have to agree with Eva, and it makes me more upset at Logan.

This is a game for him. I don't want to play a game.

This is my life. I start to get choked up, and I try to ignore it. I wish I wasn't so emotional. I wish I could just be rational about all this, but how can I be?

I'm worried this could all be a play on his part so he can humiliate me for leaving him in Vegas. His endgame could be to set me up to fail, so he can fire me and make sure I never work in sales again.

At the thought, anger and desperation mix and churn in my stomach, and a surge of anxiety rolls through me. I need to stop being scared and confront him like an adult. If Logan's plan is to humiliate me, there's nothing I can do about it but prove to him that I can handle whatever the fuck he throws my way. Just because he's my boss now doesn't mean I have to let him treat me this way.

Well, I think to myself as I signal the waiter for a to-go box so I can put my untouched food away for later, *if he wants me to play games, fuck it. I'll play.*

CHAPTER 16

LOGAN

"Mr. Parker?" Charlotte asks with an even voice and the door cracked. "You wanted to see me?" She doesn't leave the doorway though, and it forces my lips into a straight line.

I tap my knuckles on the desk and stare pointedly at the door. "Close it." My voice is low and she stares back at me with her chest rising and falling.

My command seems to trigger something in her. There's an obvious shift in her demeanor. Her eyes narrow at me but she closes it, kicking it shut with her heel and making her way toward me.

"Logan," she says in a harsh voice. She looks pissed as hell and for some reason it turns me the fuck on. My cock twitches in my two thousand dollar slacks, and my heart races in my chest. This isn't why I called her in here. I don't know what's gotten into her, but I need to fix this.

"If I'm going to lose my job over this, so be it, but I am not some office slut." She spits out the last part with venom. Is that what she thinks? Fuck! This was supposed to be enjoyable for her, and just as much as it is for me. I feel like an asshole. I should have explained things better to her.

"I am not some-"

I look her in the eyes and cut her off. "If you don't want me, there's nothing left to discuss. You still have your job, you earned it. You deserve that position."

Her forehead pinches and she opens and closes her mouth taking deep angry breaths as though she's ready to lay into me, but she's lost her steam. She wasn't expecting me to bow out of this argument so easily.

This is something she made up in her head. It's my fault for toying with her, but I didn't expect this reaction.

"If you don't want to fuck me, then don't," I say easily. "It's been two days since our discussion, and I couldn't wait another hour to see you." I stand and walk my way around the desk to her. She eyes me warily as I lean back, both hands gripping the edge of the desk.

"You aren't an office slut, and I don't see you like that at all." My eyes roam her body as I speak. "But I wanna fuck you like one," I confess to her.

Her eyes widen and she takes a half step back.

I turn to face her and take a full step forward so I'm close enough to pull her toward me, but I resist.

"I want you, Rose. I want you in my company making me proud, and I want you bent over my desk cumming on my dick."

A small pant slips past her lips. Her thighs clench, and knowing that I'm exciting her makes my dick stiffen. I reach up and slowly run my finger along her bottom lip. I can see her on her knees, sucking me off under my desk. I want that. I desperately want that.

"You're striking; it's only natural that I want you."

Her eyes stay on mine and she speaks in a low voice, "I'm not a fucktoy." There's no fight in her words though. I can see she's just as turned on as I am.

"You're not, but I think it'd be fun to treat you like one, for both of us. It doesn't have to be degrading..." I trail off and watch as her eyes fall to the floor before continuing, "unless you want it to be."

Her beautiful blue eyes snap up to mine and I can see she still wants to fight the sexual tension between us. She doesn't want to give in to the primal needs that she has.

"Today for instance," I start to say, turning away from her and walking back to my desk. If she wants this, she's going to have to prove it to me.

I sit easily in my chair as she stands defensively across the desk.

"Today I wanted you to play my secretary. I dreamed of fucking you on my desk." I put my hand out in front of me. "Right here," I say as I pat the desk and maintain eye contact with her. "It's a fantasy I've had before, but I've never fulfilled."

She scoffs at me. "I don't believe that for one second." Her defenses go up and her eyes light with a passion to prove me wrong. It pisses me off. I'm not a liar, and I've never given her any reason to think I would lie.

Before this day is over, I want her on her knees, begging me to forgive her and choking on my cock.

"I've never and I never will lie to you," I say with a lowered voice.

She stays mute, refusing to believe me but not offering me a rebuttal.

"I thought you enjoyed me fucking you." Her small hands ball into fists. "It certainly seemed that way when you were screaming my name."

"Fuck you." She practically hisses.

"Yes, please do," I say back to her with a small smile.

It's quiet for a moment, the two of us at odds. Pointless really, we both want each other. She just needs to let go and give in. I can give her pleasure while she fulfills my needs.

"This isn't a game to me," she finally says. She's not angry though, which is what I expected. She sounds sincere, and genuinely upset. "This is my life."

I grind my teeth, hating that I'm unsure of what to do. I

want her. And I'll have her. But not yet. She needs something from me before she's going to give in. It's a challenge that I readily accept.

I clear my throat and sit up straight in my seat. "Is there anything else you wanted to talk about?"

She stares at me in an attempt to calm herself down. I want to walk over and pull her into my embrace, to soothe her worries and tell her everything is going to be alright. But right now she's hostile. It would only make matters worse.

"I'll see you in forty minutes then, Miss Harrison." She nods quickly and turns on her heels.

"Rose," I call out her name and she stops with her hand on the doorknob, but she doesn't turn around. "My door is always open for you. If you decide you need anything." I hear her take in a deep breath. I'm not sure, but I think she may be crying. It fucking shreds me. "There's a bathroom to your right, if you need it before leaving my office."

She shakes her head and mutters, "I'm fine."

But she's not fine, she's so far from it.

CHAPTER 17

CHARLOTTE

God, he's driving me insane.

I walk into the bathroom around the corner from Logan's office and grab a handful of toilet paper from the first stall to blow my nose, feeling a cauldron of emotions bubbling inside. Anger, shock, lust and sadness. I don't know what to make of Logan. At first I thought he made me the head sales rep just to humiliate me. Now I'm having doubts.

What's worse is that I want to take back these last few days and play along with his game. I just want him to take me and fuck me like his office slut. How fucked up is that?

I feel ashamed thinking this way, but when he started talking dirty to me in his office, it was all I could do to hold my ground. I wanted to give into him right then and there, get on my knees and let the image he described come to life.

This is wrong. I shouldn't be entertaining these feelings. I'm so confused by what's happened. But some things are very clear. Logan is my boss now. A relationship between us would be inappropriate.

I wrap my arms around myself, squeezing tight and trying to clear my head.

Why do I have to resist? No one has to know about our relationship. It could be our little secret. A giddy grin comes over my face at the thought. *Don't I deserve this after what Ian did to me? Why can't I use Logan for pleasure just like how he wants to use me?*

... 'cause then I'll feel like a whore.

"Damn him," I growl, blowing my nose and throwing the paper towel in the wastebasket. I'm torn and conflicted. I don't know if I can trust what Logan's offering, and I don't know what to do. I sure as hell know what my body wants though. That I can't deny.

I blow out a deep breath. For right now, I need to get myself cleaned up. I can't miss this meeting.

The board meeting is stuffy, and I'm finding it hard to focus while an intern named Harold gives a presentation about a new method of advertising online. I should be paying attention to what he says, but all I can think about is Logan.

The way he looked at me in his office, with a hunger that was almost palpable and how much he wanted me, is doing crazy things to my body. The way he said, "fucktoy." The memory sends shivers down my body.

Unconsciously, my gaze is drawn over in his direction. My breath catches in my throat. He's staring back at me with a ravenous hunger in his eyes. My clit throbs in response and a prickly sensation goes up all over my arms. Not here. My heart beats rapidly. Not with everyone else watching. My eyes dart around the room, but everyone's looking at Harold.

Doesn't he know that you shouldn't mix business with pleasure?

Oh, he knows, I tell myself, *but he doesn't give a fuck. He's a man that wants what he wants, and everything else be damned.*

Logan continues to stare at me, his eyes boring into me like I'm the only person in the room. I shift in my seat, my core heating from his gaze alone. Good God, I'm not sure how I'm going to get through this.

"So how much will this new tactic cost us?" Logan asks, his eyes still on me.

It takes a second for me to realize that he's talking to Harold, and I feel a small twinge of disappointment.

Harold, a pudgy younger man with a balding head, beams happily, pleased to have caught the interest of his new boss.

"Practically nothing at all, sir," he says. "It's a pop-up, and it won't cost more than the small yearly fee of an ad."

My ears perk up, and I tear my eyes away from Logan. "That's not true," I argue. "Using this method will result in a huge loss of revenue. Studies have shown that buyers are less likely to buy and checkout when a pop-up occurs." I turn my gaze back on Logan. "It pisses them off, and they get turned off by it."

Harold goes red in the face. I can tell that I've embarrassed him, and I cringe internally, but I can't help it.

I'm not going to let someone propose an idea that would be bad for the company. I could have eased into it, but it had to be said.

"That's not true," Harold objects, shaking his head. "Layman Corp uses this very same method, and they've seen profits grow by two hundred and fifty percent."

I open my mouth to set him straight, but then stop. I'm not sure if this *debate* with a coworker in front of a room of executives would be a good look. But I know what Harold is saying isn't factual and could prove disastrous for our sales department.

Logan catches my eye and gives me an imperceptible nod.

"But were pop-up ads all they did to increase revenue?" I ask, my voice picking up confidence as I speak. "Or is there a bigger picture that you're not looking at?"

Harold stands there, glaring at me angrily.

"You do realize Layman Corp utilizes various tactics for their ads, one of which is testing ad methods that are proven to be bad for business to see if they can improve them, right? They released a study just last month that backs up my claim that they are dismal for business and through testing pop-up ads they came up with a more effective ad campaign, and *that* is what caused their profits to grow by two hundred and fifty percent."

I take in a breath, hating that I feel like I'm arguing. I don't want to. He can read the study, and this conversation would be null and void.

"Charlotte's right," Cary Ann pipes up from at the end of the table, brandishing her work tablet and drawing Logan's gaze. It's been several days since I last saw her, but she looks like she's had a long night, judging by the bags under her eyes. Her red cashmere sweater and white dress pants look nice on her, though. "There have been several studies done that show pop-up ads only piss off users, and some have actually resulted in lawsuits."

Logan swivels back around to appraise Harold who's looking like he's about to blow steam out of his ears, his face red as a tomato. I feel sorry for the poor guy. And I didn't mean to embarrass him, but I know I'm right in this.

"Is there anything else you would like to add, Harold?" Logan asks easily, seemingly unaffected.

For a moment, it looks like Harold's going to start yelling at me and branding me the demon bitch from hell, but instead he shakes his head and says, "Thank you for listening, sir." And he returns to his seat.

Close by, Eva gives me a thumbs up. She thinks I've done a good job, but I feel horrible. I didn't want to step on anyone's toes, and I'm pretty sure I've just made a new enemy. Great.

For the rest of the meeting, several people get up to speak and I do a better job at paying attention, but I catch Logan gazing at me every time I look at him. I spend awhile thinking about what just happened before the meeting and what it all means. A part of me wants to apologize to Logan for how I treated him, and how quick I was to accuse him of being an asshole. Another part of me wants to just quit this job and run away from this stress.

When Logan dismisses the meeting, I grab my briefcase and get up to leave, intending on putting everything behind me, but I freeze when Logan issues a command. "I need a moment to speak with you, Miss Harrison."

Holy hell. Not again.

Slowly, I lower myself back in my seat, anxiety twisting my stomach. I'm not sure what Logan could want with me, but whatever it is, it can't be good. Not with what happened earlier.

I sit there, my pulse picking up speed as everyone slowly files out of the room. Eva is one of the last to go and she sends me a flirty wink as if to say, 'he has the hots for you, girl' and then she leaves the room and I'm all alone with Logan.

God. If only she knew.

CHAPTER 18

LOGAN

I can feel her eyes back on me. She's back to being lost in thought as the meeting wraps up. She's so beautiful and intelligent with a poise I admire. Yet I've damaged that. That's what I do, it's what I'm good at.

I'm not used to giving a fuck. But I brought her close, and I know damn well I'm responsible for that hurt look and distant stare. She doesn't realize how fucking obvious it is.

Hastings is watching her like a hawk.

They're going to think I yelled at her or did some fucked up thing to her. And I did.

I didn't realize it though.

I shouldn't be pushing this; I should show some fucking

restraint. But she's all worked up and feeling insecure because of me. Not about what's between us, but over her job. I don't fucking like that. I didn't even consider that it would be an issue.

I never considered it because it's simply not a matter I've ever had to worry about.

It's been bugging the shit out of me since she left my office. I feel like a fucking prick.

This isn't a good look for me. I really don't give a fuck about the office, but for a woman I've slept with... I don't like her thinking I was going to hurt her. It makes me uneasy. I need to make this right.

Harold Geist wraps up his presentation. He's completely deflated now that Charlotte's corrected him. She didn't mean to shut him down. She's right though. It would have been a horrible move. I was at least going to wait for his talk to be done to tell him no. But Charlotte stepping up and telling him outright how his decision would negatively affect sales only proves to me more that I made the right decision.

I don't want to lose her.

My heart twists in my hollow chest and I'm not sure that I like how strongly I feel toward her. "That's all for today." I end the meeting abruptly. "We'll reassess next week."

Charlotte's quick to stand, and I know she's going to bolt. I'm an asshole for taking advantage of my position, but I call out, "I need a moment to speak with you, Miss Harrison."

At least this time it's for her benefit, not mine. I still can't look her in the eyes. I can feel the gaze of several people in the room, but I ignore them.

I couldn't care less about them and what they think about me.

I finally look at where she was seated, half expecting her to have just left, but she's still there, staring at the pen in her hand as she taps it lightly on the table. The rest of the group files out, most people not paying much attention to either of us.

The second the door shuts, she looks up at me with a glare. "I told you, I didn't want to do this."

I hold her gaze and watch as several emotions flit across her face. But the one most evident is insecurity. She still doesn't know what to think.

What she needs is a good fuck. She needs a release, and so do I.

She's making this so damn difficult. Part of me wants to bend her over this table and take care of her like I want to. She'd feel better then. She'd be happier.

My dick hardens just thinking about it. Charlotte clears her throat and starts going on about how she wants the same respect as everyone else. Something or other that I don't really pay attention to. After all, I respect her more than most of them. Whether she wants to believe it or not.

It doesn't stop me from picturing her plump lips parted as she pants and moans in time with me leaving a bright red mark on her ass and fucking her.

Soon... if I play my cards right.

Right now she can yell at me all she wants. She can fight this and pretend she doesn't want it. I have the time.

The thought makes my eyes drop to the floor and my fists clench. It's only when I stop hearing her sweet voice that I look up.

"You weren't even listening!" she says with exasperation.

Fuck! I didn't mean that. How fucking deep am I going to dig this damn hole I'm in?

I hold my hands up in surrender as she breathes deeply and starts to lay into me again, "I don't know what you expect from me when you won't even listen to me!" Her voice is getting louder and I'm sure they're going to hear her if she yells anymore. I should probably wait to approach her again, but I'm an impatient man.

I keep my hands raised in surrender, "I'm sorry. I do apologize."

She looks at my hands and shifts uncomfortably in her seat. She grips the pen and then looks back at me. She swallows thickly and asks, "What do you want, Logan?"

"I want to take you to dinner," I say simply.

The words come out without my consent. I hadn't anticipated it. I didn't even know what I wanted to tell her when I called out her name. I just couldn't let her leave with the way we left things.

She looks at me completely bewildered, as though she

doesn't believe what I said. Her mouth opens and closes, with nothing coming out.

I only want to give her pleasure. I can see how easily it would work. She'd benefit as much as I would. But it was never meant to leave the office. It can't be... more.

This is dangerous. More for her than me. It's one thing to take her as a fuck buddy for mutual enjoyment and keeping things limited to the office. That's what I had in mind when I saw her in Vegas. Nothing more than that. But I didn't anticipate feeling... guilty.

I hurt her, and I want to make it right. I think she just needs to see me in a different light. She has me built up as the enemy. I don't want that.

I can take her out this one time. Just once. Just to smooth things over and get her naked on my desk tomorrow morning.

"No strings. No commitments. Just dinner."

"That's why you asked me to stay?" she asks with slight disbelief.

"Yes." My heart hammers in my chest as I tell her again. "I just want to take you to dinner."

CHAPTER 19

CHARLOTTE

Just dinner. That's what he says. A part of me wants to believe him, but I get the feeling that he wants more. It makes me feel uneasy, but a part of me wants more, too. I crave what happened in Vegas between us, it was the first time that I've felt anything since breaking up with Ian.

I feel like I should be telling him no and staying away. This whole relationship is wrong, and it won't end well. I just know it. But I can't resist him. He's too tempting. And I'm addicted to him like a junkie that needs her next fix.

What if he holds it over my head if I turn him down? I wonder. *This is liable to get out of hand.*

Somehow, I doubt it. But even if he doesn't, I feel like

another hookup will only cause extreme tension in the boardroom and I don't know if I can handle any more of that. Yet at the same time, it's all I can think about.

I look out the tinted window of his Aston Martin as we ride through downtown, my mind racing with all sorts of thoughts. A call comes through his car speaker, the third since we started the drive, and we've only been driving for less than five minutes.

I see him watching me out of the side of his eye as hits the hang up button on the touchscreen of the vehicle's console. The sounds of soft, classical music fills the car once again. *Beethoven.*

I'm not usually one for this type of music, but I do find that i's easing the anxiety I feel in my stomach.

"You know," I say, turning to look at him, "you can take the calls if you have to. I don't mind."

He glances over at me, and his lips quirk up into a smile. "I do. They can wait."

My heart does a backflip. Logan is choosing me over what could be important business calls. It makes me feel special, but at the same time wary. I open my mouth to say something, and then pause. I'm not sure what I should say.

How about we stop this car and you fuck me right now? I think lustfully. I feel ashamed, but not as much as I did earlier. Not when he's treating me like this. This makes things different. It makes them easier.

"Why didn't you want to see me again?" Logan asks, breaking the silence.

"I never said I didn't. It's just that I was worried about my job and-"

"I'm talking about the note... In Vegas." His voice is heavy, and I can almost feel his emotion. Pain laces my chest, and I cringe inwardly.

"Well you know what they say, what happens in Vegas…" I say, trying to make light of it, even though I feel guilty.

Logan chuckles, although it doesn't seem genuine. "Indeed. Except, I didn't stay in Vegas, and what we did certainly didn't either."

He's right about that.

The car slows at a red light and Logan looks out of the window, contemplating something. This car drives so damn smooth, it makes my Nissan Altima seem like a damn clunker. "So I was just a one-night stand?" he asks, turning to look at me.

I duck my head, wanting to hide in the backseat. "Yeah… something like that."

Silence reigns between us for a moment and then he asks, "What about an office affair? Is that a fantasy of yours?"

Oh boy, I think to myself. *I have a lot of fantasies, and I know you could fulfill every last one of them.*

I want to say yes and tell him I'll be his office slut, his whore, his… whatever he wants me to be, but I can't find the strength to voice the words. Shit. I feel so damn conflicted about all this.

"It doesn't have to be anything more than sex, Rose," he tells me softly.

I suck in a breath filled with emotion. I love the way he calls me Rose. It makes me feel... special. But it couldn't just be sex for me. Not now. I feel too... I'm scared to admit.

The light turns green and he drives up several blocks before turning into a recently paved restaurant parking lot. It's a large, modern-looking building and looks like it cost a pretty penny to build.

This is probably where all the rich folk go, I think to myself. A small thrill goes through me. I've never had a man spend more than a couple of hundred bucks on me and I'm sure Logan is about to drop that much on one meal like it's nothing. After everything, I would think I'd feel guilty about this, but I don't. I'm excited to be taken to dinner. Especially somewhere so nice. I try not to analyze it too much, looking out of the window at all the beautiful details on the building. It's late and dark, but the uplighting is exquisite.

"Don't think about it now," he tells me as he pulls into a parking space. "Let's get dinner first and then we'll talk about it."

I open my door before he has a chance to walk around and open it. Which is exactly what he was going to do, judging by the look on his face.

I'm not going to be good at this. I'm not going to meet his expectations. My insecurities grow as he takes my hand and walks me into the restaurant. I try to shake it off, but every click of my heels against the pavement brings us closer to the obvious conclusion. I wasn't bred for this like he was.

As we approach the door, he leans down and kisses my cheek, giving my hand a squeeze, "It's just dinner," he whispers. I'm caught off guard by the open display, but he seems unaffected and easily releases me, as though it wasn't unnatural at all. I'm overthinking everything. I breathe in deep as we walk through the door.

The opulence of the decor in the is breathtaking. The restaurant is sectioned off in several areas, but all the materials used in the architecture are top-notch. Crown molding lines the ceilings, the floor is paved with gleaming marble and the tables are dressed with fancy tablecloths and gold-plated silverware.

An older man dressed in an expensive suit and greying hair greets us at the door. He must know Logan well, because he greets him with a wide and genuine smile along with a handshake.

"Mr. Parker, how are you this evening?" he asks in a rough voice that shows his age.

"Very well, Jacob. And you?"

He smiles kindly, causing wrinkles to form around his eyes and says, "Just fine, sir. Let me lead you to your table." I admire the dining room as we walk through to a private room lit with dim lighting cast by a few candles that Jacob lights as we slip into opposite sides of our booth.

The candles give off a sweet, smoky scent that fills me

with warmth. It's simply gorgeous.

I hesitantly smooth out my skirt, trying my best to take it all in as Jacob asks what to start us off with to drink.

Logan answers, "Waters please, plus a large wine glass, and Cabernet?" he asks me and the two of them look at me for an answer. I nod slightly and feel like an idiot. All he did was ask if I want wine, and yet I can hardly answer. I breathe out slowly and relax. It's just dinner.

"Right away sir," Jacob says before disappearing from the room. I'm fidgeting in my seat, fiddling with my salad fork and trying my best to adapt. I can feel Logan's eyes on me, but I'm not ready to look him in the eyes.

"You're overwhelmed." Logan speaks clearly although it's formed as a question.

I answer honestly, "Yes, this is overwhelming. All of this is overwhelming."

"If you would just relax, you would be enjoying yourself." I believe what he's saying, but it just simply isn't that easy.

I bite the inside of my cheek and break our eye contact. "It's my job, and you're my boss." I try to think of a way to explain it, but he interrupts my train of scattered thoughts.

"And we both have needs. I know you feel the tension that I feel. You want me, and I want you."

"We shouldn't though." I shake my head, my eyes pleading with him to understand.

He takes in a breath to speak, but then looks over my

shoulder. I hear the door softly close and then a young waiter is at our table.

He pours a bit of wine for Logan, who doesn't drink it but nods at him to continue. I say a soft thank you and take my glass as the young man goes over the menu.

"May I order for you?" Logan asks. I'm quick to nod yes, although I'm not sure I'll be able to stomach any food. I'm full of nerves and apprehension. I take a sip of the wine and listen as he orders a stuffed chicken, beef tenderloin and salmon. I think they were three separate dishes, but maybe one is a combo. I'm not sure.

I give the waiter a polite smile before he leaves, my fingers running along the rim of the wine glass. "This is uncomfortable, Logan," I finally admit to him.

"Why's that? This is meant to make you feel more at ease."

I struggle to explain it. "I didn't know this was going to happen. I'm not used to this, and I don't understand what you really want from me." A weight feels like it's lifted off my chest as I finally say words that make sense.

Logan takes a moment to assess the words. He's giving me his full attention and looking as though he's bartering a deal. Which, in a way, he is. Finally he says, "You need to stop worrying and just enjoy yourself."

I take another sip of my wine, practically a gulp this time. I don't think he could possibly understand. I set the glass on the table and Logan's hand reaches out for mine.

"Give me tonight." His thumb brushes over my wrist in soothing circles. "One night to show you what it could be like." I stare into his eyes and want to give in. I want to feel like I did that night we spent together. I want this tension between us to disappear and be replaced with the fire I long for.

I nod my head as I hear the door open behind me and resist the urge to turn and look over my shoulder. Delicious smells flood my senses and I wait patiently for the waiter to set the plates in front of us. Beef tenderloin and salmon for him, and a stuffed chicken for me.

"Is there anything else I can get for you?" the waiter asks.

"That's all, thank you." Logan lays his napkin across his lap and then asks me, "Which would you like?"

I look between the plates, they all look tempting. "Whichever you don't want is fine with me."

He leans forward with a smile on his lips. "I want them all." He picks my hand up and kisses my knuckles. "We can have it all, Rose. Let me show you."

I utter a yes, caught in his trance, and give myself over to him. Just for tonight.

CHAPTER 20

LOGAN

I open the door and gently place my hand on her lower back, leading her into my home. Up until now, I've been a gentleman. I've shown restraint so I can ease her into this.

As soon as I get her into bed, *she's mine*.

"Oh…" she says and trails off with obvious appreciation as she takes in a view of the house. It's an open floor plan and modern. I hired a designer to make it feel like a real home. In some ways it does. I've lived here for five years now, but in many ways it's more a place to sleep and shower when I'm not in the office. There aren't many personal things. Anything of real value to me is in my office. I have a room attached with everything I need to stay late there. At first that spare room felt like a hotel. But it quickly reversed. Now this house is the rarity and feels new and cold when I come here. And the spare room in the office is where I spend most nights. It's where I'm comfortable.

I take a look at Rose as she appraises the modern space, but I don't give her much time to look around. There's only one room I'm interested in her getting acquainted with.

I close the heavy front door and lock it, tossing my keys on the front table.

I wrap my arms around her small waist and pull her curvy body into mine. I breathe in her scent and whisper into her hair, "Wait till you see the bedroom."

She laughs a little at my joke and easily tilts her head as I kiss along her jaw and then down her neck. Her hands grip onto my arms, her blunt nails digging into my skin as I move lower, rocking her gently and taking full advantage of this view of her breasts.

"Logan," she moans, and it's the last straw. I pick her small body up and carry her up the stairs, taking them two at a time.

I've never worked so hard for a lay in my life. But I know it'll be worth it. She'll be worth it.

She holds onto my neck tightly and gasps at first, but then her eyes focus on the dip in my throat and she kisses me right there and then up my throat. Each kiss makes my dick harder and harder. Her passion is addicting.

I'm desperate for her by the time I place her gently onto my bed.

"I want you naked," I breathe as I unbutton the top button of my shirt and then rip it off and over my head. She's quick to undress as well. It's tit for tat until we're both naked and breathing heavily. Her eyes are clouded with desire as she takes in my naked body. They widen as she sees my dick, hard as a fucking stone and just for her.

I climb on the bed and it groans with my weight. She backs up slightly and gets onto her knees. She licks her lips, her eyes focused on one part of me. I don't waste a second to grab a fistful of her hair at the base of her skull and guide her lips to my cock.

She doesn't hesitate to take it into her greedy mouth. As she swallows my cock down her throat my head falls back. Fuck, she feels so good. She tries to take in more of me, hollowing her cheeks. I look down with my eyes half-lidded as she bobs up and down my length.

I could watch her all fucking day, but I want her pussy. I wanna hear her moaning my name and prove to her that this is worth it. That she didn't make a mistake by giving in to me.

I pull her off of my cock and she looks up at me with a heated gaze as she wipes her mouth. She has no shame. I fucking love it.

"Knees." I release her and she only hesitates for a moment. I can see she's debating on whether or not she's going to give me control. But she makes the right decision, spreading her legs slightly with her ass in the air. She's bared to me and glistening with desire.

I run my fingers down her spine and farther down to her wet pussy. "So fucking wet," I say as she softly moans into the sheet. Her hands move to either side of her head and she grips onto the sheets as I push my thick fingers into her. Fuck, so tight, too.

I pump my fingers in and out of her as her back arches and her head falls against the mattress. She bites down on the sheets to muffle her sweet moans. But I don't want moans, I want *screams* of pleasure. I want her to call out my name like she fucking needs me. Like I'm her everything.

I slowly pull my fingers out of her and bring them to my lips to clean them off. I practically moan as I taste her on my tongue. So fucking sweet.

I grip my dick and stroke it once as she looks back at me with a passionate gaze. She whimpers in need, but I have every intention of giving her what she needs. I push the head of my cock easily through her pussy lips and slowly move forward. Watching as her pussy takes in more and more of me. I'm slow and deliberate. My eyes move from her cunt to her face. Her lips part wider and wider, and her forehead pinches as I push deeper and deeper into her greedy pussy.

She writhes under me as I near the last few inches of my thick cock and her head thrashes side to side. She starts to move under me, but I hold her hips still.

"You can take me, Rose." She moans with a mix of pain and pleasure I push all of myself into her. Her hand grips her breast and she bites down on her lip. I gently still deep inside her, letting her adjust before pulling out slowly and then thrusting back in to the hilt.

She lets out a loud moan and looks back at me with a mix of fear and desire.

I do it again and this time there's only pleasure. She rocks her hips with arousal leaking from her pussy onto my thighs. I move my hands to her hips and steady her as I pull almost all the way out and then thrust into her. I keep this up over and over in a steady rhythm.

"Fuck!" she screams out as I pound her tight pussy. Her body jolts with each thrust and she struggles to stay still and take it, but she does.

I keep up the relentless pace until she's trembling beneath me and whimpering with her impending orgasm. Her walls tighten around my cock, and I know she's close.

I angle my hips so I hit her clit each time, giving her more and more pleasure and enough to take her over.

I groan in utter rapture as I rut between her legs. Her pussy spasms on my dick as she screams out her release. Fuck, yes. She feels so fucking good. I can't stop as I ride through her orgasm.

Her body goes limp and her pants get louder as I continue

to fuck her like I own her body. Like she's mine.

I thrust into her warmth as a tingling sensation starts at the bottom of my spine and flows through me in every direction. My toes curl and I know I'm going to cum as my balls draw up, but I don't want to. I want more of her. I almost slow down, but the threat of losing the high makes me pick up my pace.

I strum her throbbing clit with a desperate need for her to cum with me. The hardened nub is soaked. So are her thighs, and each pump of my hips is accompanied by a wet smacking noise. I fucking love it.

"Again," I growl into her ear, my voice so harsh I hardly recognize it.

In an instant she obeys. And the feel of her pleasure pushes my own over a steep cliff. I thrust myself all the way to the hilt, feeling her tight walls pulsing around every inch of my cock. Thick bursts of cum leave me in heavy waves. My back arches as she screams out my name and I give her everything I have.

As the waves dim and she lowers herself to the mattress, her chest rising and falling frantically, I pull out slowly and quickly climb off the bed and head to the bathroom to clean up.

I take my time and watch her from the corner of my eye through the ensuite's doorframe. She lays still on the bed, looking completely spent.

I'm quick to clean her up and then I toss the cloth into the hamper in the bathroom.

I walk back into the room ready to pass the fuck out. It's late, and I'm exhausted. I stop short when I see her reaching for her clothes on the floor, with the blanket held close to her chest.

"I think you'd sleep better in a tee shirt," I say and look to my dresser, knowing she could easily wear one of my undershirts. "Although I'd rather you were naked." I let my eyes fall to the bit of her cleavage still exposed. "I *much* prefer you slept naked."

"I think maybe I should go," Rose says quietly. My body goes cold for a moment. It's late. Very fucking late. And a part of me was looking forward to having her available to me in the morning.

"Do you *want* to leave?" I ask her as I walk slowly to the bed and stand next to her. She looks at the bra in her hand and doesn't respond. I cup her chin in my hand and force her to look at me. "Or do you think I want you to go?"

Her lips part slightly, and her eyes tell me everything I need to know.

"I want you to stay," I whisper against her lips and then kiss her gently. "I want you here naked in my bed, and I want you to use me for your needs. And I want to do the same to you." It's the truth. Every word.

She blushes and gives me a soft smile, pulling out of my hold. "Well, I wasn't sure how needy you were," she says playfully. It brings a smile to my lips.

She looks good in my bed, but this is an exception. The reminder makes me question if I should bring that detail up now. I imagine it won't go over well. This... *relationship* needs to stay at the office. We can't get close, this is just sex, and limiting the arrangement is the best way to ensure it doesn't get out of hand.

As I climb into bed and debate on telling her just that, she beats me to it.

"Don't expect me to be at your beck and call. I don't think sleepovers are the best thing for this..." She doesn't finish her statement, and I simply nod as she motions between us.

Although I was going to tell her the same damn thing, I don't like hearing it. And I sure as fuck don't like that she said it first.

I should be happy about it. But I'm not. And that could be a problem.

CHAPTER 21

CHARLOTTE

What the hell have I gotten myself into?

I look out the window of Logan's stretch limo as it rolls through the downtown streets back to my apartment, thinking about the night before and trying not to bite my fingernails. The whole morning I've been struggling with the feeling of regret. For having an affair with my boss. It sounds stupid for even thinking of it that way, but it's his power of authority over me that makes this so uncomfortable.

Our little tryst was definitely mutually beneficial. I'm just not sure if it's a mistake.

At least I get to drive home in luxury. Although it's one of the reasons I feel cheapened. I can't even make eye contact with the driver. I'm sure he's not thinking the best things of me right now.

I need to make a choice. Either accept this lifestyle and our arrangements, or cut it off. I swallow the lump in my throat. The lines are drawn and I have a better understanding of everything. But I'm still unsure. It won't be just sex for me. I can't imagine this ending well.

My eyes meet the driver's as we slow in front of my apartment.

"Here we are Miss Harrison," he says easily.

I give him a warm smile and say, "Thank you." I wish I could remember his name, but I don't. I climb out and wince. I'm sore and aching, all thanks to Logan. My smile grows. It's a good feeling, being deliciously used. I shut the door and give the driver a polite wave.

As I walk up to my apartment, I slowly feel better. I think it was just the drive maybe? The idea that it was a walk of shame of sorts. But being back here and knowing it was my choice makes me feel more at ease with the decision. The keys clink in my hands as I unlock the door.

I freeze when I open the door, nearly passing out onto the floor.

Ian and Sarah are sitting on the living room couch, practically making out. Sarah, who's dressed in the skankiest outfit I've ever seen, has her hands on Ian's crotch, rubbing it like it's a pot of gold and Ian is running his hands all over her body.

What the fuck?

They stop when they see me standing in the doorway, glaring at them with a mix of hatred and shock. My gut reaction is to scream at them and tell them to get the fuck out, but I know better. Ian isn't going anywhere, especially with Sarah here, and he's more liable to throw me out than to sit there and listen to me badmouth him.

"Do you mind?" Sarah snaps nastily, her hand still on Ian's crotch. Tears prick my eyes. She was my friend for so long. My grip on the doorknob tightens as Ian grins at Sarah, kissing her on the forehead as if she's done a good job snapping at me.

I grit my teeth and then bite my tongue, chanting internally to myself to stay calm, cool and collected. Ignore the pain and be the bigger person. I need to call the fucking landlord again, too.

Fuck this. I don't have time for this. I need to get to work.

It takes everything in me, but I manage to tear my eyes away from them and I continue on to my room. Behind me, I hear them say something about me and laugh. I just ignore it and go about getting ready for work.

I take a quick shower, scrubbing my skin harder than I should and am dressed in my business attire within fifteen minutes. My hair's damp, but I just throw it into a bun. I have an hour-long drive anyway, so it can dry on the way.

I stare at myself in the mirror, not wanting to go back out there. I don't want to have to deal with this. When I finally decide I have to get the hell out and walk down the hall, I hear banging sounds coming from the second bedroom and Sarah moaning at the top of her lungs as if she wants the entire world to hear.

I ball my hands into fists, anger threatening to overwhelm me. My jaw clenches, and I'm overwhelmed by all the emotions consuming me. I'm not going to cry. I refuse to cry and scream and give them the reaction they're hoping for. I'm not going to give them the satisfaction and engage them with their bullshit.

In fact, I'm over this. I take confident strides to the front door and I don't look back. Fuck them. I'm moving on with my life. They can have each other.

Grabbing my briefcase, I walk out of the apartment, Sarah's pleasured cries trailing me, with one thought on my mind.

I guess I'll be applying for that temporary housing after all.

I drive to work and I'm pissed the entire drive, my mood dark and gloomy. I hate the fact that they got to me. I'd be a liar if I said I was unaffected, but I plan to remedy that very soon. The first chance I get, I'm putting in for temporary housing.

The image of them going at it will haunt me for some time, so I'm going to have to busy myself to forget it. I refuse to let those two assholes fuck up my day and distract me from my job.

Wearing a scowl on my face, I walk inside Parker-Moore and make my way up to my office. There's a stack of papers waiting on my desk when I walk in and I feel like it's just what I need. Bury myself in work, and at the same time bury Ian and Sarah. A win-win.

I set my coat and purse down and go get coffee from the break room before returning to look through contracts and emails.

Over the next half hour, I find myself immersed in work and I lose track of the time. I'm just finishing up working data into a sales graph on my laptop when my cell rings.

"Just when things were starting to get good," I grumble in annoyance. Busying myself in work has made me feel much better and it reminds me of how much I love my job. It's been the perfect antidote to forget about Ian.

For a moment, I debate ignoring the call. It can't be anyone important, but curiosity gets the best of me. I pull it out and glance at the caller ID. Anger surges through my chest. It's fucking Ian.

Why the hell is he calling me?

It annoys me that he's back in my mind after I'd just managed to to get him out of it. Scowling, I tap the ignore button on my phone and toss it to the side. I don't know what Ian wants, but I really don't care. I'm done with him.

I try to get back to work, but now I can't focus. I'm too

irritated. Ian had no business calling me, and it's brought back that dark feeling that was finally starting to go away. I find myself wishing I had something or someone to make me forget my awful morning.

Logan.

The thought of Mr. CEO fills me with desire and pushes Ian out of my mind. The session we had the night before was mind-blowing, and I can't help but wonder what he's doing right this second. Is he working, busy running his company? Or is he up in his office, thinking of me?

I hope he is, I think to myself, feeling my core heat, *and I hope he's hard as a fucking rock.*

The thought elicits a soft moan from my lips and I squeeze my legs together. This is why this relationship with my boss is bad news. Next thing you know, I'll be bringing a vibrator to work.

I should go see him, I tell myself. But I'm not sure of what I'd even say. We've already crossed the line, mixing business with pleasure, and I'm not sure what's going to happen. Maybe I should let it go and just let him make the next move.

The ring of my cell breaks me out of my thoughts. I pick it up and check the screen. Ian. Again. [It rang earlier, so I changed it to ring...]

"Fuck off," I growl, tossing the phone back down. I don't know why I just don't block his number.

I spend the next few minutes trying to get back into the

groove of studying sales data, but I give up and start going through my emails instead. Responding to them takes less focus, and at least I'll be able to get something done.

As I'm finishing up answering the last one, I receive a visitor.

"Hey chica, what's shaking?" Eva chirps, sticking her head in the doorway. As usual, she looks sharp in a pearly blouse and black slacks, a glossy belt wrapped around her trim waist. Her hair is down today and is styled with voluminous curls. It looks good on her and makes her big eyes seem absolutely huge. On top of that, she's sporting a huge smile on her face that says she's happy-as-fuck about something.

"Nothing," I mutter, sitting aside my work laptop. "What's got you so chipper today?"

Eva steps into the room and begins wringing her hands excitedly. "You know that deal I've been working on?"

"Yeah?"

She does a little victory jump. "Well, I got it!"

I get up from my seat and go over to give her a big hug. "Congratulations Eva, I'm so happy for you!" I really am. She's been working her ass off over this. I give her a tight squeeze.

"Thank you!" Eva grins at me as we pull back from each other. "We've gotta go out and celebrate!"

For the first time in hours, I smile a genuine happy smile. I am definitely getting drinks with Eva and letting loose.

My desk phone rings before I can answer, and I hold up a finger to Eva. I need to take the call in case it's a client.

"Why the fuck are you ignoring me?" Ian snarls. "Couldn't handle seeing me happy, huh?"

Anger burns in my chest and I grip the phone so tightly I fear it might crack. It's hard keeping my emotions in check, but I somehow manage. This gives me comfort. I feel like I'm in control now. I take a deep breath and calmly say, "Just leave me alone, Ian. Please. I'd appreciate it if you just forgot my number. I don't want to ever see or hear from you again."

"You act so pissed, like I did something so horrible to you." Ian argues. "When it's obvious you bear some responsibility for what happened, hell, you brought all this on yourself."

Again I feel a surge of anger, but it's weaker than the last. This man, if I can even call him that, is someone I never really knew. Why should I let anything he does or say bother me? His words are designed to bait me into a screaming fit, and he knows what he's saying is utter bullshit. I'm not going to play into it. He's not fucking worth it. Not anymore.

I look at the doorway and mouth an apology to Eva. Her eyes are full of pity, and I hate it. I shake my head and close my eyes. I am at last done with Ian. Forever.

"You never loved me, did you?" I say to him. "You were just using me this whole time, pretending to be something you weren't." I don't know why, but saying the words out loud shatters my last defense. I feel raw and vulnerable, but in a way, stronger for admitting the truth. I open my eyes as Ian goes off about how I wasn't there for him, saying things that are mostly falsehoods designed to get me worked up. But I'm no longer listening.

Bye, Ian.

Tiredly, I drop the phone from my ear and lean over to hang it up.

At that moment, I hear a small sound near the doorway and I look over. My heart skips a beat. It's Logan, standing behind Eva... and he's staring at me with a pissed off expression.

Oh shit. I don't know what all he heard me say, but this isn't what it looks like. My heart beats frantically, and I try to think of how to explain it. But it's too late.

Before I can think of what to say, Logan turns and walks off.

Chapter 22

Logan

I know my driver, Andrew, is waiting out front of the building. I stare out of the large windows and look down. I need to go. There's more work I can do here. There's always more work, more deals and emails and business ties. But I want to leave and get the fuck out of here. I'm pissed.

She told me she was single, and I believed her.

I clench my jaw and try to relax my fists.

The way she was talking to him didn't fucking sound like things were over between them. I don't like it.

I don't like that I feel lied to. More than that, I don't like my reaction. I wanted to pin her down and fuck her while he could hear her on the phone. I wanted to show her who she belonged to. And that's dangerous.

She doesn't belong to me. That's not what this is supposed to be. I can't deny what I'm feeling though. And I fucking hate it.

I haven't gotten one productive thing done since I walked in on that phone call.

I breathe heavily and turn away from the window. I feel like a caged animal in this office. I need to find a release.

I look back at my computer screen and feel a small pang of guilt.

It's a record of her phone calls and texts. It wasn't quite legal to do, but it was easy. And I needed to know.

My father used to do this shit to my mother. I don't want to be like him. I hate falling into his old habits.

When he looked at her messages though, he found plenty. All I'm seeing is evidence that they're over.

It doesn't make me any less angry. I don't like her getting worked up over him. I want all of her passion. Every last bit. That fucker doesn't deserve an ounce of it. If she wants someone to yell at, I'd rather it be me.

I've been obsessing over that thought since I've realized it's true. I shouldn't want it.

It's well past five and this floor of the building is silent. Everyone's gone home, so I'm certain Charlotte has already left. I may drop by her office.

I crack my neck and ignore the pings from my computer

and the direct messages on my screen. I have a heavy duty punching bag in my basement. It's for moments just like this.

I've never thought of myself as a selfish man. Cold at times and distant, sure. I have flaws. Not selfish though.

But I am when it comes to her.

As if my thoughts brought her to me, a timid knock sounds at the door and then it slowly opens to reveal my Rose. I stand behind my desk and wait for her to enter. The air is thick with tension as she slowly shuts the door and finally looks up at me with those sweet blue eyes.

"Hey," she says and her voice is soft and she's twisting the bit of hair hanging along her shoulders from her ponytail around her finger. I've never seen her look so insecure in my life. Her eyes dart around the room as she stands in the doorway.

"I-" she clears her throat and then looks me in the eye. "I just wanted to clear up what that conversation was about down there."

My body's tense and I feel on edge. I'm not giving her anything. I want to hear what she has to say. "Go on," I say simply as I walk to the door and lock it.

"I... Ian and I," she starts and takes an unsteady seat on the leather sofa in my office. It makes a soft sound as she settles into it. She clears her throat and sets her purse on the floor.

She looks uneasy. It makes me feel off balance. I like knowing how things are going to play out. I set the terms,

I decide how it ends. This little prick is making me have doubts. Ian is going to pay for that.

"Your ex?" I ask, as if I don't know who she's talking about. I now know everything about that fuckface. I resist the urge to take out my anger on her and instead I slip my jacket off and lay it neatly on the desk.

"Yes. Ex." She emphasizes the word and it's the first time since she's been in here that she's had any confidence in her voice. Good. The anger turns to a low simmer and I turn away to unbutton the cuffs of my shirt.

"I am completely over him." She throws her hands to the side and continues to talk with her eyes focused on the desk. "I swear, there's nothing there whatsoever." She pauses and a flash of sadness crosses her eyes. "He just... won't leave." There's a hint of desperation in her voice and her eyes gloss over with unshed tears. She fights them back and continues, "Him and my friend--ex-friend, they were there this morning and-"

I turn and face her and press, "Won't leave?"

"Yes," she says with conviction. "It's *my* apartment. It may be shitty, but it's mine. I had it before he moved in, and now he's refusing to leave."

I walk quickly back around my desk and hit the spacebar to bring the computer back to life. Ian Rutherford's information is still there.

Charlotte goes quiet. And after a moment she reaches for her purse. Her voice is tight as she says, "Anyway, I just wanted to clear that up." She sounds defeated as she stands.

"What are you doing?" I ask her.

"I'm gonna head out," she says listlessly.

"The fuck you are. You're going to go back to him?"

For a moment she's shocked, but then the anger sets in. She takes harsh steps toward me with her heels clicking loudly on the floor.

She points her finger at me and parts those gorgeous lips of hers to snap at me, but I'm quicker.

"How badly do you want to fuck him over?" I ask in a low voice.

Her hand slowly lowers and the hard lines in her face soften. She waits a moment to answer, "I just want him gone."

Yes. That's what I want to hear. No anger. Nothing for him, not even anything negative. Empathy is far worse than anger.

"You can simply end the lease."

"I-" she stops herself and goes back to being uncertain. "I need to wait on the housing."

I pick up the phone and call Trent. It's a little after five now, but he should still be here. The phone rings and rings. Finally, he answers.

"I didn't expect to hear from you after our meeting today," he answers.

I huff into the phone. The meeting didn't go so well. It's rare that we disagree, but that's exactly what happened.

"Did you call to tell me I'm right?" he asks.

I let out a small humorless grunt and choose not to answer him. I don't have the time or energy to get into that shit with him again. "I need a favor."

"What's that?" he asks. I can hear Charlotte moving in the office. She has her purse in her hands as she walks over to the wall of meaningless awards displayed in place of family photos that don't exist for me.

"I need one of the housing units."

"For Armcorp?" he asks. I bring up his email along with all the details he needs. And then I start typing everything in, including Charlotte's current address.

"Yes," I answer as Rose turns back to face me. Part of me expects her to object. She's not one to hand over control so easily. But she doesn't.

"I have an employee that needs to be moved in by tomorrow morning. I want a moving truck there now, her lease ended, and everything in place by tomorrow."

"I'll need her-"

"Sent," I answer, hitting the enter button and sending him all her information.

Charlotte walks over to my side of the desk and I'm quick to shut off the screen and turn to her in my chair.

"Can do, anything else?" Trent asks. My Rose sets her purse on my desk and sits easily on my lap.

"That's all."

"You're going to tell me I was right and you were wrong

one of these days, Logan." I smile into the phone.

"I wouldn't hold your breath if I was you." I wrap my arm around Charlotte's waist and pull her in closer. "I have to go."

"Good night, Logan," I hear him say as I slowly set the phone back down on the hook.

Charlotte leans closer to me, her lips close to mine.

"Thank you," she barely whispers. "You didn't have to do that."

"I don't have to do a lot of things; I do them because I want to."

She closes her eyes and presses her lips to mine in a sweet kiss. "Thank you." She pulls away and looks down at her purse. "Are you doing anything tonight?" she asks, a little uncertain.

"What do you want to do?" I ask her, leaning back to take a good look at her. "Because right now I wanna take you home and fuck you until you don't remember him." The words slip out so easily, I don't want to take them back. They're true.

"I don't want to wait until we get home," she says, her voice full of lust.

She leans in for a kiss, but I put my finger up and press it against her lips.

She blinks twice, and her breath falls short.

A slow grin slips into place. "I want you naked first." She smiles, the perfect picture of sweet sin, and nods.

"Yes, sir," she answers, moving her delicate fingers to the

buttons on her blouse. My cock responds instantly, hardening at her delight in my request.

I slowly push the blouse off her shoulders. The thin material falls into a puddle on the floor and she shivers as my fingers trail down her arms and then back up.

"Stand up, Rose." She slowly slips off my lap and waits expectantly. I love this submissive side of her. She's exactly what I crave.

"Strip." She obeys, with confidence in every move. Her lace bra falls to the floor revealing her small rose petal nipples, already hardened. Followed quickly by her skirt and thong. My breathing comes in heavy as I watch her slowly reveal every inch of her gorgeous curves to me. She steps out of the skirt and intends to pull off her heels, but I stop her and pull her hips toward me.

"Leave them on." I lean forward and suck her pebbled nipple into my mouth. My fingers dig into the flesh at her hips and her head falls back as she moans softly. I twirl my tongue around her hardened nub and pull back slightly with suction, my teeth grazing her skin. I release her with a pop and grin at the red mark I caused before doing the same to the other side. Her hands tangle in my hair and she pulls slightly, causing a hint of pain that makes my dick that much harder.

When I'm done I take her breast in my hand and rub my thumb along her sensitive nipple. She moans my name with desperation and puts her hands on my shoulders.

"You're so beautiful," I say with a hint of awe. I reach down and cup her pussy. Her heat and arousal make me groan. "And fucking soaking for me."

I stand quickly, the chair rolling backward as I unzip my pants and pull my dick out. I can't take my eyes off my Rose. She bites down on her lip as she sees my cock come out on full display. "Bend over," I say, giving her the simple command. She's quick to turn as if I'll change my mind if she doesn't obey fast enough. She's eager for this. Thank fuck, 'cause so am I. Her upper half lays easily along the desk with her hands at the sides of her face.

I stroke my dick once and line up my cock at her pussy. I could go gentle, but I want her to feel this for as long as possible.

I slam into her and she lets out a cry, her hands shoot forward and she pushes a stack of papers off the desk. They flutter in the air and fall to the floor as I quickly pound into her pussy again and again and again. Her fingers grip the other side of the desk. My own grip both her hip and the nape of her neck. I can barely breathe as I mercilessly thrust into her slick heat over and over again.

She screams out with every thrust although she's trying desperately to silence them. I fucking love it. I want everyone to hear it.

I've wanted this since I laid eyes on her. Me fucking her over my desk. I'm still fully clothed, but she's bared for me. I slam into her harder, wanting more from her. Needing to hear her scream my name.

Her nails scrape along the desk, trying to hold on and her head thrashes to the side.

Her hips crash across the desk and refuse to give her any escape.

Her body stills and trembles as she sucks in a breath and I know she's close. I pick up my pace and give her everything I have. Needing to cum with her. I need it as much as she does.

Her lips part as she screams out my name. Her pussy spasms around my length. My breath comes in quick pants as I pump into her again and again, loving how tight her cunt is as her orgasm rips through her. Finally my toes curl and waves of pleasure rocks through me. My head falls back as thick streams of cum leave me. I push in short shallow thrusts until the final wave has passed and I feel like I can breathe again.

Her eyes close and her head falls limp to the desk with her heavy breathing. I love seeing her spent like that. I want it again. And again.

I quickly tuck myself back in and grab a tissue off the desk, wiping up the cum from her sweet cunt and tossing it into a bin.

I kiss the small of her back and then playfully nip her earlobe. She shudders and gives me a soft smile. She's sated and exhausted, still lying how she was while I took her. "I want you tonight. I want you available and ready whenever

I want you." I'm still hard. I should take her again now. The thought of having her in the back of my limo stops me. She finally props herself up slightly and looks back at me over her slender shoulder. "Tonight?"

I nod a yes and say, "You can stay at my place tonight."

So much for keeping things separate.

CHAPTER 23

CHARLOTTE

W*hat the hell am I doing?* I ask myself.

I'm sitting at the bar in Logan's kitchen, engaged in thought, while he readies the dinner table. Our hot lovemaking session worked up a hunger and Logan ordered Chinese takeout on our way over. Yet with how my anxiety is growing, I'm not sure I'll be able to eat by the time it arrives.

I feel like I'm losing control. This whole thing with Logan is supposed to be mutually beneficial, friends with benefits, but I'm starting to think that it's more than that. At least to me. I can see it growing to that already. And that scares me. It terrifies me that I think I'm falling for him. Especially when I feel like this is still a game to him.

I wrap my arms around my torso, squeezing myself tightly, feeling a range of emotions. I'm not sure agreeing to stay at his place for the night is a good idea. Not when I can't trust my feelings. I should tell Logan that this is starting to be a problem, but I feel anxious about how he might take it.

He says this is just sex, just for our enjoyment and nothing else. And God, am I enjoying it. But I'm starting to feel that it's more than that. Much more. And I'm afraid if I tell Logan, I might drive him away. As much as I feel like a relationship with him is a bad idea, I don't think I'm ready to lose what we have. I don't want to lose *him*.

And maybe I'll never be ready.

"What are you thinking, Rose?" Logan asks me as he finishes setting the table.

I snap out of my pensive thoughts, focusing my eyes on his gorgeous face. He's studying me with a look that's intense and at the same time brooding.

"I was just thinking about how absolutely gorgeous your kitchen is," I lie. Though I'm trying to hide my emotion, I do have to admit it does look like a grandmaster chef's paradise with gleaming quartz countertops, stainless steel appliances, and tons of space to whip up gourmet meals.

I give him a weak smile and add, "I get the sense that you don't cook very often, though." I'm choosing to just ignore everything that happened in the office about Ian. I think it's better this way. It actually brought out a side of

Logan that makes me feel comfortable and secure. But that's what's causing this new insecurity. I'm just moving from one problem to the other. For a moment I feel pathetic. But then I look up at Logan. It's because of these men.

Logan shakes his head. It takes me a moment to realize he's answering my question about cooking.

Of course he doesn't cook, I say to myself. *The man could hire a score of personal chefs to cook for him. Why would he go through all the trouble?*

"Seems crazy to order takeout when you have all," I gesture expansively at the grand kitchen, "this."

Logan, walks over to me and I feel the beginnings of desire stir, along with a dull ache from where I'm sore. He's just so irresistibly sexy. I never stood a chance. "Would you rather cook for me then?" He nods back at his huge, state of the art, stainless steel refrigerator. The damn thing even comes equipped with a touchscreen and WiFi. "I'm sure there's something in there to make... somewhere."

"Me?" I snort. "Sure... if you want to end up dead on your kitchen floor."

Logan lets out a dry chuckle. "I bet you're being too hard on yourself." He leans against the island's granite top. "Your cooking can't be all that bad."

"Trust me, one taste of my cooking and you'd be changing your mind in a heartbeat."

Logan laughs again and the rough sound combined with

the sight of him so at ease and happy stirs an emotion in my chest. I suddenly feel a wave of apprehension as the feelings I've been struggling with threaten to overwhelm me. I try to push it all away, but it stays with me.

I tap my fingers on the counter and try to ignore them. The soft *click, click, click* of my nails aren't soothing though. For the past few hours, things have been better that way, with me ignoring the constant insecurities and red flags going off in my head. Yet I feel like if I don't get what I'm feeling off my chest, things are only going to get worse.

Just tell him, if he gets spooked by how I feel, then this wasn't meant to be.

The notion that he'd cut me off as soon as I tell him that I might be feeling more for him than the sex fills me with dread. But I'm burning with the need to put this out there. I want to get a feel of where we're at. And it's not going to happen if I keep pretending like this is all just hot sex.

Summoning my courage, I say seriously, "Logan."

Logan's expression is solemn as he looks at me, and I get the sense that he already knows what I'm going to say. "Yes?"

I hesitate. This is it. This is where I tell him how I feel, and it'll be our last night together. "I'm... scared," I say finally. There. I said it. If he pushes me away after this, so be it.

Logan doesn't seem at all surprised by this admission. In fact, it seems like he's been expecting it. "About what?"

My heart pounding, I gesture at the space between us.

"About this. About us. I feel like this could... become more than just sex for me."

Logan walks over and climbs onto the stool next to me, taking my hand and kissing it softly, sending tingles up along my arm. Then he looks me straight in the eye. "I appreciate you being honest."

Searching his face, I wait for him to say more, to tell me that this is becoming more to him as well. But he doesn't say it, and instead he looks like he's calculating what he wants to tell me, like he wants to be very careful of what he says next.

This fills me with wariness, and it's just another red flag that I'm better off leaving, yet I remain glued to my seat.

After a moment, Logan offers, "How about this. Let's just enjoy each other for as long as we can, and if everything goes well, we can reassess later?"

It's not the words I want to hear. I'm telling him how I feel now, and if I'm already feeling like I'm too invested, what's it going to be like later? Will he just keep stringing me along as I slowly fall in love with him, using me as his sex toy until he wants to discard me?

It's an unsettling thought and not one I want to believe he's capable of doing. But the fact that he isn't starting to feel the same is yet another warning sign. I shouldn't be here. And I need to get out before I'm in too deep. I just don't know how.

"I don't know if I want to do that," I say. "I don't know if I can handle another..." my voice trails off. *Ian.*

Logan stares at me and I feel like he wants to say something, but is holding it back.

My lips part to ask him what it is that he's not telling me, but the sound of the doorbell interrupts the moment. Our food is here. Planting another kiss on my hand, Logan gets up from the bar and goes to pay for our meal. I take a deep breath as he leaves the room and try to shake out my nerves. On top of being sore from our fuck session, I'm tense all over.

This is going to end up not working, I tell myself. *I'm going to end up heartbroken and all alone, my faith in men shattered.*

I don't want to believe this. I want there to be something between me and Logan, as there's so much more to him than sex. But there's a reason why he doesn't want to become more involved, and I need to just accept that.

I need to just tell him that after tonight, this is over. There's no reason to string this along if it's never going to turn into anything. I'll just end up a messed up basket case.

"What can I do to ease your mind?" he asks me as he sets the bags down on the counter and takes out one white takeout box at a time. The smell fills the room and although my mouth is watering, I don't have an appetite. He takes my hand in his and I feel like just melting in his arms and telling him, *Tell me that you feel the same way.* Without that, I'm not sure I can, or should, move forward.

But I can't say the words, because I know I'm just setting myself up for disappointment. Logan knows how I feel and if he wanted to put me at ease, he could just simply say that he feels the same as me, even if only to get me to shut up. The fact that he hasn't shows that this is as far as he wants it to go.

"Outside of assuring me that you won't leave me for feeling like I want more out of this relationship," I say over the lump in my throat, "nothing."

I wait for him to tell me that he won't abandon me if I get too attached, but he sits there silently with that apprehensive look again. It's like he's afraid, but of what? I'm the one with more to lose here while he's a goddamn billionaire that can have any woman he wants and I'm just his little fuckdoll that he can choose when and where to have.

Anger burns my sides and I snatch my hands out of his. Why the fuck am I still sitting here? He's all but telling me that this won't ever be anything more than just sex, and I'm just being stupid by thinking it will ever be anything but.

"I think I should go," I say and swallow the lump in my throat and slip off the stool to my feet to leave, but Logan holds me in place.

"Don't go," Logan says simply.

"Why? I mean nothing to you." I'm surprised by the hurt in my voice. He *shouldn't* care about me. This was just supposed to be fun and games. No strings attached. It's not his fault that I've reneged on the contract and am wanting more out of this.

Logan looks like he's about to say something, something

that he's been badly wanting to say, but he swallows it back. "That's not true at all, Rose."

"Then why?" I ask. "Why can't you... say that... that this is going somewhere?"

Logan stares at me for a long time and I wait with bated breath. "We just need to give it time," he says finally. "I just don't think you know fully of what you're getting into."

What the hell is that supposed to mean?

"What do you mean by that?" I ask warily. "I know exactly what we're doing. And I know where it's headed."

Logan looks at me, and I see pain in his eyes. "I understand," he says finally in a grave voice.

It shatters my heart that he can't give an inch. Especially when I just opened up to him like that.

He takes my hand and pulls me close, and I'm enveloped by the heat of his hot body. I don't want to move away. I want the comfort. I need it.

"You just need to relax, and live in the moment. I want you. I don't want you to leave. Not yet." The pained look in his eyes is replaced by a desire that's hard to resist.

"But what-" I begin to protest, but he kisses me on the lips to smother it.

"Just give in, Rose," he whispers, slowly bringing his lips down to my neck and nibbling softly.

Every cell in my body is telling me to push him off me and demand that he tell me why he'd rather pretend this situation is going to get any better, but I'm overcome by his advance. I tilt my head back and my lips part into a soft groan as his hands move up my thigh.

"We don't need tomorrow," he murmurs, delivering another scorching hot kiss to my neck while undoing my skirt, "just tonight."

Chapter 24

Logan

I take another look at my phone as the driver pulls up to Charlotte's new place, the temporary housing I arranged for her. It's been nearly two weeks. And more than half the time, she's stayed at my place. She's staying here tonight. Her decision, not mine. I'm glad she's the one who brought it up. She can't come back with me tonight, but luckily I didn't have to tell her.

She's typing away on her laptop. Busy with her new ventures in the marketing research department. She's doing well. I glance up at her as the faint sound of her tapping on the keys stops. She leans back and reads whatever it is she wrote out, or maybe something else, I'm not sure.

She looks so beautiful though. Her hair is down from the ponytail it was in and it flows in soft curls over her shoulder. There's still a faint blush to her cheeks from our early adventure in the office. She's becoming a bad habit of mine. Although Trent seems to think I'm more amicable now that *something's changed.* He obviously knows judging by the way he smiles when she knocks on my door.

I look back at my phone. There are other people who know, too.

I should tell her about the photo and the message. There's nothing in the photo that's scandalous, nothing that's harmful. Just a picture of the two of us leaving Parker-Moore. She's walking beside me as we approach the limo out front. Anger rises within me. I don't like her being watched. I don't like her having a target on her back.

She deserves to know. But I don't want to give her a reason to stay away. She's right to be cautious. But not for this reason. Not for some asshole who thinks I'm *screwing the secretary.*

It's an innocent enough photo, but the message is what pisses me off. And the fact that someone thinks they can fuck with me. I just don't know who. I will though. Maybe then I'll tell her.

She seems to only just now notice that the limo has stopped. She shuts her laptop and slips it into her bag, unbuckling her seat belt and getting ready to leave me.

As she double checks that she has everything, including a

dry cleaning bag of three of her outfits she's left at my place, she gives me a small smile and grips everything in her hands.

"I'll go with you," I offer.

"No, don't," she says stubbornly, "I've got this." She leans forward and plants a kiss on my lips and pulls back slowly. At the same time my phone beeps and vibrates in my hand with a text.

It catches me off guard. Maybe it's my nerves. She seems to realize I'm off a little, but before she can think on it, I pull her closer to me, one hand on her lower back, the other on the back of her head and slip my tongue along the seam of her lips until she parts for me. The dry cleaner bags ruffle as she drops them to run her hand through my hair. Andrew starts to roll up the partition and I let out a small chuckle.

Charlotte backs away and leans down to grab her bags.

"I'll see you first thing tomorrow." She nods and slips out of the limo. It's not until she's in her building that I tell Andrew to head home.

"Thank you for that, Andrew." His eyes catch mine in the rearview mirror and he smiles.

"No problem, sir."

My home is only fifteen minutes away and I spend the time looking out of the window and watching the people walking along the busy streets of downtown. Couples holding hands and laughing, a few men and women in power suits and brightly colored pencil skirts talking on their cell phones and walking at a quick pace and brushing past the slower walkers.

The world keeps moving. No matter what happens, it's merely small ripples for the most part.

I don't even realize we've traveled up the hillside to my house on the cliff of the city, until Andrew clears his throat.

"We're here, sir," he says, looking back at me in the mirror.

"Thank you, Andrew." I quickly grab my briefcase and make my way inside. Before I push the large maple door open, I turn to my right and see the doctor's car parked in the circle driveway.

My heart sinks. I have these visits. I grit my teeth and try to forget everything else. This must be done.

Marilyn greets me at the entrance. The front entrance has a fresh citrus scent and there are fresh flowers in the vase on the entryway table. Signs of her work.

"Hello and goodbye, Mr. Parker," she says with a small smile.

"Good night, Mrs. Doubet." I leave the door open for her.

She says in a quieter voice, "The doctor is in the great room, waiting for you."

I give her a tight smile and nod. I answer, "Thank you."

She doesn't respond, instead she ducks out and leaves to go back to her family or maybe somewhere else. I watch her leave and then close the door behind her, leaving my briefcase on the table.

I take off my suit jacket and unbutton my shirt as I walk straight to the great room.

It's my favorite room in this house. It's why I bought it. The back wall is lined with floor-to-ceiling bookshelves. The dark wood shelves and chair legs are freshly polished, shining from across the room and the faint of smell of citrus fills my lungs. There are two large tufted sofas and a grand fireplace made of slate. The thick red curtains covering the large windowpanes are always drawn back, giving the room a more open feel.

I haven't lit the fireplace in God knows how long. As I walk across the room to the leather chair that the doctor's pulled out for me, I realize I haven't been in here since the last time he came for a visit. Two months.

It's my favorite room, but on these days I hate this fucking room.

"Doctor Wallace," I greet as he hears me walk into the room and turns to face me. He's an old man with a slight hunch to his back and thick glasses that cover his pale blue eyes. He doesn't look quite like a doctor in slacks and a red polo that looks like it should be worn by a younger man.

I take the seat and slip my shirt off, tossing it onto a nearby end table.

He gives me a small smile and nods. I'm not one for small talk. He's used to getting this over with quickly.

"Anything new since we last met?" he asks me as he puts the stethoscope to my back and then tells me to take in a deep breath.

"No changes." I say the words, but internally I feel like a liar. She's new. My Rose.

My fingers touch my lips and I remember the faint sounds

of her moaning in my mouth.

It would be nice to have her home with me. But not tonight. She can't be here for my appointments.

At the thought I take my phone out of my pocket, remembering the beep from the text earlier. It's Trent. Doctor Wallace pulls away, giving me space to look at it.

My heart stills as I read through the message.

That fucking bastard. I stand instantly with barely contained rage.

Chadwick Patterson. That fucking prick. Trent traced the message, or had someone else do it for all I know. But he's certain the message is from him.

He's going to fucking regret it.

I think for a moment about how I can get back at him. This isn't the first time that he's tried to fuck with me. He's pissed the division of Parker-Moore went to us. The Parkers. He was an heir to it in his head. As Moore's bastard. But when that old man died, it was all left to my father. The business anyway. Patterson was given a chunk of inheritance, but not a damn bit of the business. So he quit. Made a fucking scene on his way out, too. He wasn't happy with a job, he just wanted a stake in the business. He's a fool and I've never paid much attention to his antics. But it's one thing to fuck with me, and it's another thing entirely to bring my Rose into this.

"Mr. Parker?" Doctor Wallace asks as I pace in front of the open windows.

I shake my head. "I need a moment."

I see him take a seat from the corner of my eye. I pay him well. Damn good money. He can wait a moment longer.

He's going to have some sort of consequence to make it damn clear that he needs to back off. I've looked over his businesses and I know there's going to be a soft spot somewhere. I need to find it. I need to find a way to hit him where it hurts. As I scroll through the businesses listed on his company directory on my phone, I try to remember the conference and which talks he attended, who he was trying to negotiate with.

A smile creeps to my lips. I know he settled on a new business with Arrivol. Their manufacturing plant is in horrible condition and he placed a bid on the old Chrysler plant. I put two and two together and know exactly how to fuck him over. Worth a few billion at least.

I dial up Trent, knowing exactly what to do.

"You got my message," he answers on the second ring.

"I did. And I want to fuck that bastard over where it hurts."

"Calm down, Log-"

I cut him off, I don't need to calm down. "I want the plant on Levington." I stop walking and stand in front of the far window. It overlooks protected woods that are a part of the city park. It's peaceful, elegant even. It's everything I'm not.

"We can use that in the-"

"I don't care what we use it for. Patterson *needs* it."

"I'm sure it's a silent bid," Trent says after a long moment.

"I don't care how much it's going to cost to win that bid. If you have to overspend, do it."

"By how much?" he asks.

I snort into the phone. "I don't give a fuck if you spend another four million on the property. Patterson needs it or he's fucked, so fuck him. Make sure he doesn't get it. Is that clear?"

"Understood," Trent starts to say something else, but I'm done talking. My blood is pumping with adrenaline and I can feel anger boiling beneath the surface.

I hang up the phone breathing heavily and squeezing the phone with rage.

"Mr. Parker," Doctor Wallace says, snapping me back to the present.

I clear my throat and nod, setting the phone down and walking back over to the chair in the middle of the room.

"You should take it easy; stress isn't-"

"I'm fine." I cut him off and try to calm my racing heart.

"You're not fine," he says, walking over to the large bag he placed on the table. He looks back at me through his spectacles. "You need to keep that in mind, Mr. Parker."

I take in a slow breath and nod.

For nearly three years it's been on my mind every minute that I'm not working. I've never been able to ignore it. My heartbeat slows and I retake my seat.

Until her.

My Rose. Such a beautiful distraction.

CHAPTER 25

CHARLOTTE

I stride confidently down the hall to Logan's office, my heels clicking against the gleaming hardwood floors. I'm dressed in a white blouse and a tight black skirt that shows off my curves; I want to look good for my boss. For the past few weeks, this has become a regular thing for me, and I no longer feel anxious about meeting Logan without an appointment.

I look forward to it even though I still question our relationship. I know it's stupid, falling for a man that doesn't want to commit, but I can't help myself. He makes me feel good. Valued. Even when I do get pissed off with him being evasive about us being together, he's always able to deflect my ire with passionate kisses and a good hard fuck.

If I was smart, I'd leave him. But it's too late. I'm addicted to him, mind, body and soul. And worst yet, I think I'm falling for him. Hard.

As I pass his receptionist's desk, I nod at his secretary, Eleanor. She's an old lady, probably in her mid-seventies with stark white hair that she always wears in a severe bun. She returns an imperceptible nod. She's so used to seeing me show up unannounced that she doesn't even bother greeting me anymore.

I'm sure she's wondering what's going on between me and Logan, and why I have special access to him, but most of the time, I don't give a fuck. Logan is a man that gets what he wants, and he wants me. Still, I'm uneasy about being so bold about our relationship, even if it's only his secretary who suspects something is going on. It's only a matter of time before the whole building knows, and I'm not sure how they're going to react when they find out.

When I get to the oakwood double doors of Logan's office, I pause, my heart racing.

Why do I keep doing this? I know this isn't going to end well. He's all but admitted he wants to continue to take this one step at a time and won't guarantee I won't end up with a broken heart.

It's a pointless question, because I can't help myself. I *have* to see Logan. He's become a necessity, like food or water. And there are no guarantees in life.

He's told me not to knock, but I don't like just busting in on him at moment's notice. I think a little heads-up is the polite thing to do. Taking a deep breath, I gently rap on the doors.

"Come in," I hear Logan's muffled command.

I open the doors and walk in, but nearly trip before I do, closing them behind me. Logan's on the phone, but goddamn he looks sexy as fuck. My heart beats faster and I unconsciously lick my lips. He's sitting in his tufted leather office chair, wearing a black dress shirt, his red tie loosened at the collar, his shirt open at the chest. His hair, which is usually gelled and slicked, is kind of messy, like he just woke up.

My core heats with desire at the sight of him.

He looks up at me as soon as I enter. "Hold, please" he tells whoever it is on the other end of the line. He drops the phone to the desk without waiting for a response.

He always makes them wait... just for me.

This is why I can't leave him, I tell myself. *He makes me feel more important than any man I've ever been with.*

"Rose," he says, standing from his desk and stalking toward me as I make my way to him. His eyes are narrowed and heated, staring at me as though I'm his prey. But I walk straight to him, and let him devour me.

He's quick to wrap his arms around my waist, pulling me toward him and making my back arch as he kisses me with a heated passion I can't deny.

I lose myself in his embrace as our tongues intertwine, massaging against each other with intense need. I fall back against his desk, my skirt rising up my thighs. Fuck. He can take me right here. Right fucking now.

Before I can shove his shirt off of him and reach for the buckle of his belt like I so desperately want to, Logan pulls away from me and I gasp, my chest heaving. Slightly embarrassed, I straighten up and pull my skirt back down, my thighs trembling.

"We can't," Logan says quietly, smoothing his slacks. I can see his large hand pressing against his dick and readjusting it, and my mouth waters at the sight. "And I think I'm going to have the worst fucking case of blue balls when the day hasn't even started yet."

"Sorry," I say breathlessly, straightening my outfit.

"I'm good," Logan says. His voice lacks his usual fervor. "I'll make sure you make it better later."

The way he looks at me tugs at my heartstrings, and for a moment, I want to bring up our situation again, tell him how much my feelings have grown even after several weeks. But I realize this is not the time, nor the place. It can wait till later.

"Can we do lunch?" I ask instead. I've been having a hell of a time being wined and dined at all the expensive restaurants on Logan's dime. I've almost forgotten what it's like to go through a drive-thru. "Maybe fast food for once?"

Spearing his fingers through his messy hair, Logan takes a moment in responding and I feel a twinge of concern. "I have to take a raincheck," he says. His eyes have a worried look in them and he glances at the phone, something he never does. Usually he'll leave them on hold so long they hang up.

"Of course," I say, doing my best to hide my disappointment. I feel slighted, but I shouldn't. Logan has literally made time for me at all hours of the day. I can't expect him to keep doing this forever. It would be selfish of me.

Still, I can't help but wonder, *Is he getting tired of me? Is this the reason why he didn't want to commit, because he knew that this day would come?* I clear my throat and try to ignore my quickened pulse and the feeling of dread washing over me.

It makes sense. Now that Logan's had his fill, maybe he was ready to move on. The idea frightens me more than I'd like to admit.

Logan dampens my worry with a soft kiss on the lips, but his demeanor remains solemn, almost sullen. "Thank you. I promise I'll make it up to you."

As excited as I was to walk into Logan's office, I'm starting to feel tense. This muted welcome is worrying. "I'm going to hold you to that promise."

"I have absolutely no problem with that." He pauses and looks at me, noting my subdued mood. "You sure you're going to be alright having lunch by yourself?"

I flash a weak smile. Something is definitely off with Logan, and I don't know what it is. "Yeah. Actually, Eva's probably looking for company, so I'll just hit her up." I need to talk to Eva anyway, I've been putting her off since getting closer to Logan and we have a project we're working on. I take out my phone and send her a quick text.

Me: Hey chica, lunch?

I look up to talk to Logan, but he moves around to his desk and shakes his mouse to look at the computer screen. My phone pings.

Eva: Yup, where at?
Me: At the Blue Cafe on the corner.
Eva: See ya there.

I put my phone away. "I'm gonna meet her at the Blue Cafe."

Logan relaxes. "Good. Do you want to use my limo?"

I shake my head, though I'm pleased by the offer. It'll raise Eva's eyebrows if I showed up in a limo to a cafe that was just two blocks from the building. She probably already knows what's going on. I get the sense that a lot of people do. Still, lately I'm feeling different about keeping my relationship with Logan a secret. If it weren't for his reluctance to have a real relationship, I'd want the world to know.

But the way he's acting now has me wondering.

"No, I'll walk." I step forward and give him a quick peck. "Thanks for offering though."

"And thank you for being so understanding," Logan says

before picking up his phone. "Are you there? ...Alright." Logan gives me a distracted wave as I leave, and I can't shake the feeling that something is wrong as I walk out of his office.

Outside it feels good, a cool breeze sweeping up the street. The sky is clear, and the deep blue color would take my breath away if I wasn't in such a sour mood.

If this is the beginning of the end, then it will be no less than I deserve. I knew I shouldn't have gotten involved with him.

I make it halfway down the block, lost in my thoughts and hardly watching where I'm going, when I feel a prickling sensation on my neck. Someone's watching me. I turn around, scanning behind me. There are a couple of people walking on either side of the street, entering businesses, and cars driving by, but no one stands out.

For a minute, I continue to scan, my eyes darting everywhere, but I eventually give up.

After a moment, I turn and continue on, thinking, *Relax, Charlotte. You're just being paranoid.*

"Did you see what happened with that celebrity guy in the news?" Eva asks me as she takes a bite out of her blueberry bagel that's covered with cream cheese. We're sitting in the Blue Cafe in the corner. It's been awhile since I've eaten in a place that has a dollar menu, but I'm happy to see Eva and catch up on corporate gossip and talk about the project we're working on together.

As usual, Eva's dressed sharp as a tack in a red pantsuit and matching lipstick, her hair pulled back into an elegant ponytail. I need her to be my stylist.

I pause, peeling the plastic wrap from around my banana nut muffin. I'm trying to be cheerful with Eva, but I just have a bad feeling. I don't like how distant Logan was with me in his office. "What guy?"

"It was what's his face," Eva snaps her fingers together multiple times trying to jog her memory, "the hot young guy that plays a president on that one show and he cheats on his wife with an intern." She motions at me as if I'm supposed to be a psychic and give her the answer. "You know, *that* guy."

Actually, I have no idea who *that* guy is. I'm drawing a blank. Since starting the new job, I don't watch much TV, and the only hot guy in my life is Logan. "I don't know who you're talking about-"

"Jake Goldwater!" Eva yells and slaps her hand on the table. "That's it!"

I vaguely know who she's talking about, I think I've watched a few movies he's been in. I don't think he's anything special. "What about him?"

"Well supposedly, in real life he also heads his own company, Goldwater Productions." She taps a finger against her chin thoughtfully. "I think he even owns a building several blocks from here. Anyway, he got caught banging one of his secretaries... on video."

"Damn," I mutter, shaking my head. "I'd hate to be that girl. She'll be humiliated for the rest of her life."

Eva gives a short laugh. "You'd be one of the only ones. There's probably scores of women who'd sleep with him on camera."

"Good for them," I mutter darkly.

Eva bringing up Jake's scandal hits close to home. The parallels are freaky. I'm not Logan's secretary, but I am sleeping with him. It makes me feel ashamed that I just don't come out and tell Eva. I almost feel like a fraud.

It would be nice to have someone to confide in, someone I can tell my doubts about Logan to. Someone who can tell me that I'm insane for staying with a guy, even if he is rich, that won't commit.

Eva peers at me with concern. "Something wrong?"

"No," I lie. "I just feel overwhelmed with all this work." *And worried about the direction my relationship with Logan is going.*

"Aren't we all." Eva pauses and she looks like she's debating on whether bringing up a topic.

"Speaking of hot bosses, there's a rumor going around about Logan..."

"Eva," I say, cutting her off. Here's my chance to come clean with Eva. At this point, it'll be a relief. With all my doubts about our relationship, I don't see a reason to hold back anymore. I just hope Eva doesn't judge me too harshly.

She shakes her head, setting aside her bagel, her face twisting with shock. "Oh no, don't tell me..."

"I've been sleeping with Logan," I say super fast. There. I was right. I feel so much better already.

Eva's mouth opens wide with shock. "Jesus, Charlotte, how long has this been going on?"

I tell Eva everything, about Vegas, about sleeping with Logan and then leaving him. I hold nothing back, and when I'm done, I feel even more liberated. "After Ian, it was so easy to just fall in bed with him. He was just so charming and... sexy. I couldn't help myself. But now I'm worried that we're..." *Finished.* I feel a lump form in my throat at the thought.

Maybe I'm just overreacting and it's all in my head.

That's what I want to believe, but deep down inside, I know otherwise. That Logan's hiding something from me, I'm certain, I've just been doing a decent job in deluding myself that things will get better.

Eva's shaking her head in disbelief and doesn't seem to notice my last sentence. "No wonder he gave you the head sales position."

"So you think that's the only reason I got the sales job?" I ask irritably. I thought Eva would be giving me relationship advice, not questioning my position in the company.

"Don't you dare," Eva says defensively, seeing that I've taken her words the wrong way. "You know I would never think so lowly of you. You're a beast at what you do, and everyone knows it. That's why Logan hired you." The passion and sincerity in Eva's voice make me feel ashamed for jumping to conclusions.

Eva shakes her head. "What I *meant* is that Logan wanted you, and seeing how good a sales rep you were, he made sure you'd work closely with him."

"I'm sorry, Eva," I say softly. "I didn't mean to snap at you."

Eva waves away my worry. "It's no problem. I woulda got pissed too and thought the same thing if I was in your shoes."

She pauses and then gives me a look. "So is everything okay with Logan? You sounded like you're having some serious issues... despite the good sex."

I let out a sigh. "He won't commit. He just tells me we should live in the moment. But I don't know what to do... I think I'm falling in... falling for him. And I'm afraid that I'm going to end up..." My heart clenches and I take a deep breath. It's so hard to admit.

Eva grimaces. "That's... not good."

"Yeah, and I'm not sure how much more time I should devote to something that's never going to work out. Even if the sex is good. I don't want a repeat of Ian, you know?"

Eva nods and makes a face. "Yeah, but ugh. It sucks because you're at a disadvantage in this relationship. Like, he can totally get rid of you if you suddenly decide you've had enough and want to break it off with him."

Eva isn't saying anything I haven't already considered,

and it's depressing. I'd like to think that Logan would never do such a thing to me even if we did break up, but then I remember Ian. I thought I knew him, thought I'd marry him and have his children even, and he turned out to be a totally different person than who I thought I'd fallen in love with.

When it comes down to it, I don't really know Logan either.

"So what are you gonna do?" Eva asks, her expression deeply concerned. "I'm afraid to give you advice on this because I don't see a clear answer." She leans forward and takes my hand in hers and gently adds, "I just don't want to see you hurt."

The answer should be easy. Stop wasting time. Leave Logan no matter the cost. But when I think about leaving him, I feel overwhelmed. I don't want it to have to end. Yet I hate being in this state of limbo.

"Charlotte?" Eva asks when I don't answer right away.

I sigh and squeeze her hand before letting go. I take a bite out my muffin, shake my head, and reply, "I don't know, Eva. I really wish I knew."

Chapter 26

Logan

My eyes are drawn from my computer to the large doors of my office at the sound of a loud knock.

"Come in," I call out. I half expect it to be Rose even though it's a quarter to five and I doubt she'll be done with work this early. I want it to be her. But it's not, it's Trent.

As he closes the door, I stretch my arms above my head and sigh heavily. It's been a long fucking day.

"Did we get it?" I ask as he slumps into the sofa and leans forward, his elbows on his knees with his chin resting in his hands.

He nods and says, "It cost us forty-three million. But we won the bid."

I finally let a grin slip into place.

"We overspent, but it's still usable," he says.

I huff out a breath, the smile unmoving. It feels good knowing how badly I fucked over Patterson. And he's going to know. There's not a damn good reason for me to have bought it otherwise.

"Logan," he says and waits for me to look at him.

I raise my eyebrows as he makes me wait in silence.

"Yes?" I ask him, finally leaning forward and giving him my attention.

"Are you alright?"

He hasn't asked me that in quite a long time.

"I am." I clear my throat and look at the clock and then back to him. "I'm fine." I'm not fine. But I'm not as bad as I once was. I know that's why he asks. I can run this company. He's the only one who knows about my condition beyond my father. If it got worse, I'd tell him. I wouldn't let the company fall.

"That's not what I mean."

I look back at him with my forehead pinched in confusion.

"It's about Miss Harrison."

"Charlotte Rose." I feel my hands grip the arms of the chair. My blunt nails dig into the leather. "What about her?" I ask, my voice on edge.

"Is she-" he stops to look away and then back at me. "Is this serious?" he asks.

I wait a moment to answer. I know the truth though. It

is. I've never been more serious about anything in my life. I want her. I need her to be mine.

"Yes," I answer and hold my breath, waiting for him to tell me all the reasons we shouldn't be together. Instead a smile grows on his face.

"I'm very happy for you, Logan." He leans back and says, "I'd like to meet her; maybe outside of the office?"

I scoff a laugh and finally relax. I nod my head, looking back at the clock. "I think she'd like that. Maybe a corporate lunch."

He lets out a laugh. "To think you have a life outside of work."

I bring my fingers to my lips. It's certainly something different. *She's* something different.

"Does she know?" he asks. My breath catches in my throat as I maintain eye contact. I don't want to answer. I can't admit to him what a selfish prick I've been.

I'm saved from responding by a small, timid knock on the door. It opens before I can respond, and Charlotte appears.

She's in a simple shirtdress that flatters her curves, and I can't help letting my eyes roam her body as she hesitantly walks in. "Are you in the middle of a meeting?" she asks in a hushed voice, gripping the edge of the door.

Trent has a wide smile on his face and answers for me. I'm caught in a trance at the sight of her. As if telling Trent she was mine somehow made it more real. More tangible. Something I can actually have.

"Not all, we've just wrapped up." He slaps his hands on his thigh and stands.

"I'm not sure we've met officially," he says and holds a hand out to her and I finally rise to walk over and help introduce them.

She accepts his hand. "Trent Morgan." She says his name with confidence and with her back straight. Her purse jostles as she shakes his hand. "It's nice to officially meet you; Logan has said nothing but nice things about you."

Trent laughs and pats the back of her hand before releasing her and says, "He must not have said much then." A small chuckle rises through my chest at his joke as I wrap an arm around her waist. It's the first time I've ever held her in front of anyone. A small gasp leaves her lips and she looks at me, nervously tucking her hair behind her ear. Her eyes flash with surprise.

"I'm glad you've met her, now get the fuck out." I say the words easily with a grin and he nods, picking up his jacket off the sofa.

"You two have a nice night," he says as he opens the door.

"You too," my Rose says in a slightly high-pitched voice.

She watches the door until it closes. And then she looks up at me and asks, "We're an item now?" Although there's skepticism in her eyes, her voice is laced with a hope I've never heard from her.

I simply nod. I don't like that she's questioning it, that

she's doubting me.

I understand, but I don't fucking like it.

"Like..." She pauses and takes in a short breath before pulling away slightly and then looking back at me. I keep my feet bolted to the ground and wait for whatever the hell she's thinking to come out. "Like people can know?"

I huff a small laugh and walk over to her, she refuses to believe me. "Yes. The world can know you're mine."

"Do you mean it?" she asks in a soft voice that displays her vulnerability. I hate that I ever made her feel so insecure.

I nod and whisper back, "Yes." Her body relaxes somewhat, but she doesn't respond.

"Do you want me, Rose?" I ask her, turning her in my arms and pulling her soft body into mine. "Because I sure as fuck want you."

She braces herself with her small hands on my chest as she looks up at me with wide eyes. She nods, and breathlessly says, "Yes. I want you."

I crash my lips against hers in a bruising kiss. The need to claim her has my dick hard as a fucking rock.

I pull away and tear at the sash around her dress, desperate to get it off. Her nimble fingers unbutton her dress fast enough to save it from being destroyed.

I pull back to look at her. Her tempting body in nothing but heels, a black bra and matching panties. Her chest rises heavily with quick breaths, and her face is flushed with desire.

Fucking gorgeous.

She quickly unbuttons my shirt, not waiting for me to act. I reach around, undoing her bra as she kneels on the floor, unbuckling and unzipping my pants with a desperate need. She tugs them down and releases my cock. My hands fist in her hair as she quickly takes the head of my dick into her mouth.

I groan, but I don't let her take any more. I pull her off and step out of my pants. She waits on the floor, watching me, but not for long.

I reach down and pick her up in my arms. Her lips press against mine and she parts for me. My tongue massages along hers and the air turns hot between us.

My fingers curl around the flimsy lace and I easily shred them and toss them carelessly to the floor, not breaking our kiss.

I push her back against the wall for leverage so I can move one hand off her lush ass and down between us.

I slide my dick between her folds and then roughly push into her hot pussy.

She moans loudly, slamming her head against the wall. I leave open-mouthed kisses along her slender neck as I thrust up and into her welcoming heat.

"Mine," I groan in the crook of her neck. She whimpers my name as I quicken my pace.

One of her heels falls to the ground with a loud bang as her feet dig into my ass, her legs wrapped tightly around my hips.

"Say it," I command her.

"I'm yours!" she cries out with her head arched to the side. "I'm yours, Logan!"

Yes! I slam into her over and over. Each time the wall shakes, threatening to knock the frames off the wall.

I look to my left, to the large windows covered by blinds. I grab her ass with both hands and move us to them, opening the blinds and continuing to fuck her as her back hits the cold glass.

"Logan!" she cries out, her breasts pressed against my chest as I continue my relentless pace.

I pull out of her and turn her around, pushing her beautiful frame against the glass. We're so high up I can barely make out the people below. But I want this.

"What are you doing?" she whispers, her voice laced with desire. I reach my hand around to her front and rub my fingers against her clit. She moans and tries to move away slightly. I slam my dick back into her and continue mercilessly stimulating her throbbing clit.

"I'm gonna make you mine, and the whole world's gonna see it," I growl.

"Oh, fuck," she moans out, her hot breath leaving fog on the cold glass as her cunt clamps down on my dick.

Her eyes go half-lidded and her body tenses.

"Yes," I breathe onto her neck, my lips just touching the shell of her ear. "Cum with me, my Rose," and on my command her head falls back against my shoulder and I lose it.

Everything in me comes undone as my orgasm races through my blood. I kiss her lips as my dick pulses deep inside of her.

We stay just like that for a long moment after, both of us trying to calm from the intensity of our orgasms.

I finally let her go and turn to grab a few tissues, cleaning her first and then my cock, which is still hard.

She walks to the corner and sags slightly, her legs still trembling as I gather our clothes.

I can't stop watching her as I dress myself. Picking up the now-wrinkled shirt and slipping it on as my breathing tries to steady itself. We could stay here in the office, but I want to bring her home.

"Logan," she says with great effort, finally picking up her bra and dress and slipping them on.

I smile down at her as she tries to speak. I walk over and hold her small body to mine. "Are you alright?" I ask. She leans into me and nods her head. I kiss her hair. "What did you need?" I ask.

She finally stands on her own, pushing me away slightly and pulling her hair out of her face. "Nothing," she says with a small smile, shaking her head.

She picks up her heels and slips them on, giving me a sweet smile over her shoulder. I eye her, but leave it at that. I pick up my tie off the floor and shove it into my pocket.

She picks up the lace scrap on the floor and looks at me as though I've committed an awful crime.

"I'll get you more."

"But what am I going to wear out of here?" she asks in a hushed voice.

I walk over to her and take the torn thong, tossing it into the trash bin under my desk. I lean into her, with both hands on her ass and squeeze as I kiss her, silencing her sweet squeal of surprise.

I pull back with a grin. Her face is flushed and her breathing heavy.

"Nothing," I finally answer her.

She looks at the trash bin and then up to me with a devilish smile before nodding and pulling her dress down over her ass. She grabs her purse and opens the door, waiting for me.

That's my Rose.

There's a faint sound of my secretary, Eleanor, tapping on the keyboard from the entryway of the office, but not any other sounds.

I look up at Rose as I lock the door behind us and lead the way. She's not showing any sign that she's affected, so next time I'll have to up the ante.

"Have a good night," I say and nod at my secretary, the only person left on the floor, and keep walking with the sound of Charlotte's heels accompanying us.

"Should I go home tonight?" she asks as we walk side by side to the elevators.

I'm not sure if it's because all the blood in me is still in my dick, or because I've already made decisions about our relationship that she hasn't come to realize yet, but it takes me a moment to realize that she means her temporary apartment. But I want her in my bed tonight. I'm finding that I sleep much better with her there.

"No. I want you in my bed tonight."

She looks up at me with apprehension, but nods as the elevator dings and the doors open. It's empty and quiet as I press the button for the main floor.

She purses her lips. "And my car?"

"Can stay here," I answer easily. I watch her, waiting for some sign that we're on the same page. She nods and grips her purse with both hands. She's tense.

"We can take things slow," I say, staring straight ahead.

She lets out a small laugh of disbelief.

I cock an eyebrow and smirk at her.

She smiles and leans into me, giving me a chaste kiss on the lips. "If you say so, Mr. CEO."

CHAPTER 27

CHARLOTTE

I'm completely immersed in going over contracts when the phone rings and disrupts me. The ID says it's a call from Hastings. I don't want to stop what I'm doing, so I ignore the chimes of my ringtone, but he doesn't give up, immediately calling again. Damn it. I sigh with slight irritation. I'm exhausted and I don't have time for interruptions, but this must be something important.

"This better be good," I grumble before picking up the phone and subtly clearing my throat. "Hello?" I answer in a professional tone.

"Charlotte, you finally answered," he says, voice low and carrying a tone of urgency. "I need to see you in my office. Now."

I glance at the pile of contracts sitting in front of me. "Is this something that can wait? I really need to get these last few things done..." I feel bad being so forward. "A lot is riding on this," I add.

"No," Hastings says firmly. "I want to see you this instant." My eyes widen and my heart skips a beat in my chest. Something's wrong, and I can't help that a sickness stirs in the pit of my stomach.

I'm silent for a moment, and it's long enough that he adds--

"Now, Charlotte... You need to hear about this in person."

"I'll be right there," I answer quickly and hang up. I can't shake a bit of dread.

I sigh and smooth down my chiffon dress as I walk down the hall. I feel a prick of distress as I think everyone seems to be turning to look at me as I make my way over to Hasting's office, but I brush it off due to the fact of what I'm wearing, a brightly colored dress. Still, I feel a little uneasy. The stares aren't normal.

I knock lightly on Hasting's door, my heart beating a little faster and my palms a bit sweaty before stepping in into his office. I freeze when I see who else is there. Eva. It looks like she's distressed, her large eyes filled with worry as they fall on me.

A feeling of dread runs through me and numbs my body.

Hastings nods at me, his lined face drawn and serious. "Close the door, Charlotte," he orders.

The intense feelings grow stronger and my chest starts

feeling tight.

My heart racing, I do as he commands. The door closes with a loud click and I walk over in a daze and sit down next to Eva. She takes my hand in hers, squeezing it lightly, causing me shake like a leaf in the wind. I don't make eye contact with her even though her eyes are boring into me.

Hastings leans forward across his desk, clasping his hands together. "We have a problem," he tells me.

I nod my head rather than speak around the lump growing in my throat. My heart's racing so fast it's about to beat out of my chest. There's no doubt in my mind that this is bad. *Very bad.*

I'm about to pass out, and I haven't even heard the news yet. *I'm fired,* I think to myself. *This must be it. I've just lost my job.* My mind is racing at light speed with a number of dark scenarios.

Hastings sucks in a deep breath and my eyes dart back to his, waiting anxiously. "I don't know how to tell you this Charlotte, but we... were emailed photos of you this morning."

Hastings lowers his head as if he's almost ashamed. "Of you and Logan Parker... together." His last words leave no doubt about what he means by 'together'. My face heats and my blood goes cold. I try to speak, but I can't.

Hastings turns his monitor and Eva pulls her hand away, leaving me feeling alone, but I reach out and grab onto her. She's quick to lean forward and hold my hand. I need her. I'm thankful she's here.

My heart jolts in my chest when I see a picture on the screen and I immediately start to hyperventilate. It's hard to look at and tears prick my eyes, but I don't let them fall.

Eva gives my hand another squeeze and rubs my back, but it doesn't help. I'm shocked, angry and hurt beyond belief. I can hardly breathe.

Seeing the shock and anger on my face, Hastings raises his hands out to me. "Now now, Charlotte, I want to assure you that no one here thinks any less of you." He nods at the envelope. "Do you want to see them? I know it's a horrible thing to ask, but you should know what was sent to us. Take all the time you need before you look."

I stare at the desk for a moment, feeling a mountain of shame pressing down on my chest, and then burst into tears, sobbing uncontrollably.

Immediately, Eva pulls me into her arms, whispering comforting words in my ears that I don't hear.

"We're going to help you get through this, Charlotte," Hastings tells me firmly. "I promise. Whoever is responsible for this vile act will be held accountable. I've already contacted the authorities."

His words barely register, and they do little to comfort me. The damage has already been done. I'm ruined. I'll never be able to come to work again without feeling like a cheap whore.

Shame drives me from Eva's embrace and out of my seat. I have to see Logan and tell him what's going on.

Alarmed by my behavior, Hastings rises out of his seat and reaches for me as I storm toward the door. "Charlotte, wait!"

I ignore his command and I hear Eva say something to him, but I don't catch what it is. I'm too consumed by my emotions to care. On the way up to Logan's office, I ignore the dubious stares I get. When I hit the top floor, I march past Eleanor's desk without a word.

I burst into Logan's office, swinging the double doors open wide, feeling the last bit of control I have slip away at the sight of him. Logan, who's sitting in his chair and on the phone, looks up with surprise.

"It's over," I say and my voice cracks, barely able to keep myself from collapsing.

"I'll call you back," Logan says quickly into the phone, hanging up. He jumps out of his seat and makes his way over to me. "What's going on, Rose?" he asks, pulling me into his arms. I collapse against him, a blubbering mess.

I try to tell him what's going on, but my words come out all garbled as I cry and sob. I'm a mess. I can't help it. I'm practically shaking.

He shakes me gently, trying to get me to stop sobbing. "Rose, I need you to calm down."

How can he begin tell me to calm down? There were pictures of us screwing being circulated around everywhere. I bite back my anger, he doesn't know.

"They have pictures of us," I manage to push out the

words as I pull away from him, tears streaming down my face.

"Pictures of what?"

"Pictures of us screwing!" I yell.

Logan's face turns hard as he pushes me to the side and takes large strides to the door. Several people are looking in, making my heart still as he slams it shut and turns to look at me with a deadly expression I've never seen.

CHAPTER 28

LOGAN

I close the door and lock it. Charlotte's hysterically crying on the sofa with her phone in her lap. She's practically shaking and I need to comfort her, but first I need to end the web conference. I quickly stride to the other side of my desk and type in a message that the meeting is canceled. Voices from the executives fill the speakers, but I shut off the microphone and the monitor, my heart racing in my chest. I doubt they heard. Even if they did, I wouldn't give a fuck.

She's hurt though.

Photographs.

Of us fucking... so *new* photographs. My heart hammers in my chest as the anger rises, threatening to consume me.

I'll fucking kill him. I'll destroy him and everything he's ever touched.

I walk slowly to the sofa and kneel on the floor.

I pet her hair as she wipes her eyes and looks up at me. "Everyone," she says as her voice cracks and she wipes under her eyes angrily. Her mouth stays open, but nothing else comes out.

"It's going to be okay," I say as calmly as I can.

She pushes my arm away. "It's not! How can you say that?" She looks up at me with a pained expression. "Everyone saw me..." Her face falls, and she can't finish. She manages to look away from me and the anger courses through her. Her hands ball into fists as she looks up and past my desk.

"Right fucking there," she says and points to the window. "No one will ever respect me."

She heaves in a breath and continues, "They're going to think I only got this job because-"

"Stop it." I stand up, cutting her off. "What they think doesn't matter," I say and my voice is hard and full of venom. "This will be dealt with."

"Dealt with?" she asks incredulously. "My job is ruined."

"It's-"

"I rely on presentations, I can't hide behind a computer ignoring everyone. Everyone I ever meet will have seen them."

She reaches for her phone, and my heart slows as I realizes she's bringing them up. Her shoulders rise and fall heavily as the shock and sadness leave her and anger takes the forefront.

She finally passes me the phone, angrily wiping the tears from her reddened cheeks.

I look down with the intention of it being a glance, but I focus on it. She looks beautiful, in complete rapture. Every inch of her on display. My grip tightens on the phone.

She's for me and me only.

I don't want anyone else to see that look on her face. It's for me. Anger consumes me as I throw her phone onto the sofa and push my hands through my hair. It's my fault.

"It's my fault," I can barely breathe out.

"No." She brushes her tears away, shaking her head. "This was a mistake," she says in a small voice and doesn't look me in the eyes.

Mistake.

My heart slows, and my blood turns to ice.

"Whoever did this," I start to say although I already know who. Patterson. I'll confirm it and then he's done. "I'll make sure they pay."

She rises from her seat and slowly grabs her cell phone as she heads for the door with a look of defeat and despair.

"Rose," I call to her, but she ignores me, intent on leaving. No. I stare at her, my heart thudding painfully in my chest. No. "Rose!"

"I'm sorry, Logan," she says in a pained voice, reaching for the door.

I slam my hand against the door above her head before

she can open it. "Where are you going?" I ask her as calmly as I can, although I'm not anywhere near that emotion.

"I knew I should've never gotten involved with you," she says in a soft voice that cripples me.

She tugs on the doorknob, but I lean my weight against the door and cage her body in. "Rose, don't leave."

"I have to, Logan." She stares straight ahead and closes her eyes as I lean forward and kiss her neck.

"Don't." Her voice cracks and tears slip down her cheeks. "Please, just let me go." She wipes the tears away and swallows thickly. "I need to go."

"You don't."

"I do," she says the hard words with conviction. Shaking her head, she says, "I can't stay here. This was wrong. I knew it; I'm sorry."

I can make this right. I can calm her down and make her understand that everything will be fine. But as I try to think of a way to ease her pain and have this blow over, I can't think of anything. I'm paralyzed with the fear of her leaving me. My heart slams against my chest, willing me to do something, to say something.

But I have nothing. For the first time in my life, I feel true panic and it cripples me. I'm failing her, and I know it.

"I'm sorry, Logan," she says with her eyes still closed.

"Nothing to be sorry for." I'm quick to say the words, shaking my head, completely aware that I'm in denial. She's not leaving me. She can't.

"It's over," she says as she covers her face with her hands, finally releasing the doorknob.

Her shoulders shake and I pull her closer to me, but she pushes me away, shaking her head.

She turns to look up at me with tear-stained cheeks and puffy eyes as she says, "Just let me leave."

The words resonate with me. I've heard them before. My mother told my father that I don't know how many times. I do what my father never did, and back away from her. I stare at the wall of frames and try to ignore the sound of the door opening and then closing. Leaving me alone as I struggle to breathe.

This was going to happen. It's the way these things work. I try to convince myself I'm telling the truth, but it doesn't stop the pain. I brace myself against the wall, in complete shock and disbelief. It hurts. The crippling pain brings me to my knees. I lean my back against the door, not wanting this to be real.

I finally had something I never thought I would. And I let her slip through my fingers. It's my fault. It's all my fault.

I stay in that position for I don't know how long. Letting the scene play out again and again. I finally move, but I feel as though I'm not really here.

At least she's away from me now.

I walk out of the office, and it all falls into a hush. A few phones are ringing and some people are typing, but the sounds of keys clicking dims as I lock my office door.

I don't make eye contact with anyone, although I can feel them all staring at me. This is what she went through. I fucking hate them all. I clench my hands into fists and ignore my secretary as she stands and says something. I don't hear it, it's all white noise.

I take the elevator to the parking garage. I don't even know if my car is here. I've been using the limo so I can spend quality time with my Rose.

I don't know if her car was here. I call her as I head to my car. I need to make sure she's okay.

It rings and rings. She doesn't answer.

My car's there, parked in my spot.

I get in and sit there for a moment. And then I finally put the keys in the ignition. I don't turn it on though. I keep hearing her words play in my head. It's over.

She's sorry. She knew she shouldn't have.

My head falls back against the headrest and I stare at the cement brick wall ahead of me.

I don't know what to say to convince her otherwise. I shouldn't. I shouldn't try to convince her otherwise. But what we had felt so good. So right. It felt *real*.

The sound of a car's horn from outside the garage wakes me back to the present. I finally turn the car on and drive home.

A long time passes with no sound, and I don't even realize it. I debate on turning up the volume, but I don't want to. I wouldn't listen to it anyway.

When I walk inside, my house feels colder and emptier than usual as the keys clank against the table.

Charlotte's dry cleaning is on the entry table. It's there to greet me.

I walk past it and straight to my bedroom.

I lay on the bed fully clothed and look at the ceiling. My chest hurts. My body hurts. I can hardly stand the pain. The cell phone's right there. I know where she lives. I need her in this moment. I know she's what I need.

I pick up my phone to call her, but can't press send. It's my fault he did that to her, and I can't take it back. There's no fix to this. I deserve this pain. I knew I was no good for her.

I close my eyes, hating that my actions caused her pain. That I *ruined* her.

I never thought this would happen though. Anger simmers beneath the pain. I grip onto it. Needing it and feeling alive again with it.

I'll ruin Patterson. I'll make sure he pays for what he did to her.

CHAPTER 29

CHARLOTTE

I *wish I could afford to tender my resignation,* I think to myself as I set my glass of hot tea down on my desk and peck out a response to an email. *Then I'd be gone like the wind.*

I lean back against my headboard in my PJs, working on my laptop, sitting cross-legged in bed. I'm trying to focus on getting work done, but all I can think about are the events of the past few weeks that led up to this. The pain, the humiliation. These emotions haunt me daily and makes it hard for me to focus on important tasks. I wish I could just leave. But quitting means giving up this apartment and my paycheck. I have no savings. I have to keep working. I applied to nearly sixty jobs yesterday, none of them in my field. I'll take the pay cut and start at the bottom. I never wanna go back. I take in a shuddering breath. I have to until I have something else though. At least Hastings is letting me work from home.

But he can't save me from everything; I have a press conference coming up on Tuesday, and I desperately don't want to go. I don't think I can bear it, seeing Logan, seeing all those accusatory eyes on me, knowing what they're thinking.

She's a whore, an office slut. I can just hear it now. I lean back and close my eyes.

For days now I've been weighing my options. I could quit, but there was no telling if I'd be able to find another job. By now, word of my sexcapade with Logan has spread throughout the entire sales industry. No self-respecting corporation that cared about their public image would ever hire me, and I'd probably be laughed out of interview rooms across town.

I just have to face it--I'm stuck. And a part of me blames Logan.

It hurts just thinking his name. I feel horrible for leaving him the way I did. I was just emotional and feeling alone. I've waited all week for him to call. He hasn't, and it hurts. I thought what we had together meant something to him.

I was a fool to stick around when he told me to my face that he wouldn't commit. I deserve this.

The pain almost overwhelms me and tears burn my eyes. I climb off the bed and grab a tissue from the box on my desk to blow my nose, then toss it into the wastebasket with a hundred others. I knew I shouldn't have gotten involved. I feared ending up like this, becoming a sorry, broken mess.

He should've called me, I think to myself, *even if he doesn't think I want to talk to him, to prove me wrong. To show that he really does care about me. At the same time, I should have called him.*

Even Hastings has called me, though he's kept everything professional and hasn't once mentioned the photos. I think he feels sorry for me and wants to keep an eye out, make sure I don't go try to go jump off a building somewhere.

If I can get through these next few months, I'll look for another place... in another city, I tell myself.

The thought makes me miserable and I slog through the mass of emails feeling like shit. I'm just through responding to my last email when I get a call from Eva.

"Hello?" I answer the same way I always have.

"Charlotte!" Eva cries, her voice joyful. "I'm so happy to hear your voice!"

I hold in a groan. I know she's trying to be cheerful because she knows that I'm in a dark place, but it's not going to help. Despite what she says, it's hard not to think that she thinks less of me after she saw the photos of Logan and I screwing. "Thanks," I say. "How are things going?"

There's a pause on the other end of the line and then I hear Eva suck in a breath. "Alright. Things have been going great with the project." She's not mentioning anything about the photos. Good, because I don't want to hear it. Although she did leave a message on my voicemail about it on the day after it happened and the first day I stayed home from work. I never returned that call. I suppose she got the memo.

There's another pause and then she blurts, "Hannah, Cary Ann and I are doing a ladies' night tonight. Wanna come?"

Not really, is my initial thought. I shift on the bed, pushing the laptop away and trying to get comfortable. I don't want to go, but I feel somewhat obligated because of how supportive Eva is trying to be. I know she only wants me to get out of the house and out of this depression. Yet there's no way I'm going to go and deal with the stares... the looks. I haven't talked to Hannah and Cary Ann since it happened, and I'm sure they're going to have questions for me. I can't handle that tonight. It's just too much. "I'm sorry, Eva," I say finally, "but I really don't want to."

"Please," Eva implores. "I'm just worried about you. Getting out for some fresh air and a relaxing drink would be good for you."

"I... just can't." It's obvious that we handle things differently, and she's only trying to help. But I know I won't be alright. I'm not ready to put myself out there like that.

Before Eva can reply, there's a knock at the door. "I gotta go, Eva. Sorry." I hang up the phone and crawl out of my bed, quickly jogging to the front door so they don't leave. When I get there, it's a different story. For a moment, I debate on even opening the door. There's no one I wanna talk to... other than Logan.

Instead I peek through the peephole. I see an old man dressed in black standing outside. I watch as he raises his hand and knocks again. I wait, hoping he'll go away, but he stands there and knocks several more times.

I finally answer the knock with a raised voice, "I'm not presentable right now, so I would prefer you leave and come back at a decent time."

I can barely hear him through the door, but my ears perk up when he says, "It's about Logan."

The chain lock clinks as I unlock it and I swing the door open. "What about Logan?" I ask breathlessly.

The old man doesn't answer right away, taking in my PJs and disheveled appearance.

"Miss Harrison?" he asks.

I grip the door and answer, "Yes. I would really like to get straight to the point." Even in my PJs I'm attempting to command a sense of professionalism. It's laughable, but I don't have the energy for small talk.

He nods politely. "What happened between you two," he explains, clasping his hands in front of him. "Logan's done this before. He destroyed a woman's career, and it was extremely unfortunate to watch."

I cross my arms, suddenly feeling extremely exposed and try not to let the tears pricking my eyes come. I hate how everyone knows. Worse than that, the implication this man is making. Logan wouldn't do that. I shake my head slightly, but the man continues.

"You should sue him," the old man continues. "Make him pay for what he did to you. It'll be hard for you to get a job if you suddenly find yourself unemployed, no? If you take him to court, you won't have to worry about that." I can't believe this man has the audacity to make such an accusation. As if reading my mind, he holds up his hands in defense. "I knew her well. And she was never able to recover, so that's why I'm reaching out to you. For your benefit and hers." His voice is soft and soothing. It's genuine. My heart crumples in my chest. I can't breathe. Logan... set me up?

"But why?" I barely breathe the words out.

"He has a history of hurting others for sport." I cover my mouth with my hand as my blood turns to ice and my stomach churns. No, I can't believe that. "Mr. Parker has deep pockets. I'd bet he'd settle out of court to avoid the negative press it would bring his company. And you wouldn't suffer over the damages he caused you."

When I don't reply, the man says, "I just wanted to let you know your options." He hands out a gold-plated business card to me that reads, *Johnny Black & Associates.* "Here's my card. If you decide you want to take action against Logan, call me."

He turns and walks off, leaving me standing there running my finger along the edge of his business card and struggling to understand and accept why I fall for men who only want to hurt me.

CHAPTER 30

LOGAN

I look over the email from the lawyer once more. It's on my phone as I sit in the car outside of Charlotte's apartment. I'm pissed. I can't stand waiting on the law for judges to sign off on warrants. I already have all the information they need. Although, it wasn't obtained legally and for now I need to wait. Patterson is guilty, and I'll spend whatever it cost to ensure he does jail time. I won't settle on anything less.

But for now, I need to keep my head down and talk to public relations, according to the lawyer, Joseph Casings. I sigh heavily and sit back in my seat.

I grit my teeth. I don't fucking like waiting. I can't sit back and do nothing. Which is precisely what PR told me to do as well. To carry on as though nothing has happened. And as for Charlotte, she's to do the same. Although I haven't had a moment to speak with her. She hasn't come to work, and I haven't called her without knowing how to make this right. But I know now, I have something to offer her. I only hope it's enough.

My body tenses and my heart slows as I think about how she must feel. I don't know what else to do.

I fucked up though. Although Patterson would have found a way to use her against me, it's still my fault that *this* is what happened. My ego gave him an opportunity that destroyed her, and no matter how much I'd like to deny it, it will affect her career. For awhile at least.

I sent out an email and made an announcement this morning. If anyone utters a word about those pictures, they'll be fired. No questions or excuses. The legal department has to handle the rest, but it won't be enough. Nothing can make it go away.

And now I'm sitting outside of her apartment like a lovesick puppy debating on crawling back to her and begging for her forgiveness. Debating on *how,* really. Not if I will... just the best way to go about it.

She needs to know that I'm sorry, and that I'm going to make it up to her as best as I can.

My heart hammers in my chest as I finally get out of the car and make my way up to her apartment, and again I feel that pain rip through me. I pause on the stairs and lean against the wall, waiting for it to pass. It doesn't seem right. The pain radiates in my leg. Awareness races through me. My heartbeat slows with fear. But the pain seems to dim. I hold my breath, ignoring it and willing it to leave me the fuck alone. Something's off, but it can wait. It has to wait until I've at least talked to her. I need to tell her. The pain lessens to a tolerable level, and I continue climbing the stairs with shortened breath. At the top, I consider calling Doctor Wallace. In the past two years, I've only called him once. My jaw clenches and with the pain nearly gone, I decide to let it go.

It'll be fine. I'm fine.

I walk to her door, a gold 22 on the plate on her door, and I knock three times. I take in a steady breath and nervously straighten my jacket as I wait. I can just barely hear shuffling noises from inside her apartment and then a click of the lock.

It takes a long moment of waiting with bated breath before she opens the door slowly, only a few inches at first, and then a bit more.

My Rose.

The dark circles under her eyes make my heart sink. She looks tired and unhappy. Her lips are paler than usual, and her eyes are red and slightly swollen. My poor Rose.

"Rose," I say and start to reach out to her, but she pulls away quickly and the soft lines of her face harden.

"Logan," she says, leaning her body slightly forward

and making it obvious that she's not going to let me in. I'm caught off guard. I know she left me, but this seems... uncharacteristic.

"I just want to talk," I tell her.

The expression on her face changes slightly, showing her sadness, but only for a second. A split second so fast it makes me think I imagined it.

"Talk then," she says in a clipped voice.

I swallow thickly. I didn't anticipate discussing this in the hallway. I didn't think she'd be so defensive either. I debate on asking her why, but then I think better of it. Whatever she's comfortable with will work for me. "Public relations' suggestion is to carry on and essentially pretend this never happened." Her eyes pierce into me as though they're daggers. I clear my throat and stand a little straighter.

"The lawyers are going to make sure that he pays for doing this to you." Her eyes narrow, but she doesn't respond. She's sizing me up and I can see she's going to snap at me. She's just waiting for a chance. I welcome it though. I need something from her. I'd take anything right now, but she's giving me nothing.

"I'm going to handle this, Charlotte." She stands in her doorway, pulling the door closer to her. "He won't get away with it." I'm doing my best to convey that I've done everything I can do. "I promise you." I put as much emotion as I can in my voice, but her body language is still tense. My heart squeezes in my chest.

She looks at me with complete distrust, and I don't understand it. I don't know where this animosity is coming from.

"Please forgive me, Rose," I whisper and put my hand up to push her hair out of her face, but she flinches and moves away, leaving me to let my hand fall.

I clear my throat and let the silence pass between us. She looks past me, and doesn't say anything.

"I'll keep you updated on the legal matters." Her eyes dart to mine. "We can sue him for harassment at least. I'll bury him financially. Taking away his social circle, bankrupting him, it won't be enough." My heart beats frantically as the adrenaline pumps through my veins. I will make him pay for what he did. I stare into Charlotte's baby blue eyes, but she gives me nothing in return. Cold as ice.

"I'm sure Patterson will have his legal team try to shut down the case, but my legal team is far better than anything Johnny Black can throw at me."

"Who?" she asks, with her forehead pinching, her demeanor changing slightly.

I nod my head, realizing I jumped into this without explaining much. Fuck. I wish she'd just let me in so I can talk to her without this awkwardness between us. "His name is Chadwick Patterson. He's the one who sent the emails, it was his IP address and it's not the first-"

"No, Black. Johnny Black." She says his name with a harsh edge and a bit of distaste. It's odd, he has a reputation, but I'm surprised she'd know anything about him or his shady legal tactics.

"Yes, Patterson uses Black for his legal defense and I'm sure he has him on retainer."

She looks me dead in the eye as her breathing picks up. Her grip tightens on the door as her face reddens and her bottom lip trembles with a mix of anger and sadness.

"I'm so tired of being lied to and not knowing what to think." She spits out her words with venom. She's practically shaking, and I'm not sure what to make of the situation. I put my hands up in surrender.

"Rose," I say and try to keep my voice gentle and calming, "I'm not lying to you. I've *never* lied to you."

She throws the door open and turns her back on me. The doorknob hits the wall, sending the door flying back at me. I put my hand out to keep it from shutting and cautiously take a step forward. She's not okay and she needs me, but I'm not sure what the hell is wrong with her.

No fucking way am I walking into her apartment. Not without knowing what the fuck she's doing, and whether or not I'm even welcomed.

"Rose?" I call out to her as she practically stomps to the kitchen island and snatches something off the counter.

She walks back to me with a deadly look. "This Johnny

Black?" she asks, her voice accusatory, with a raised voice, shoving the card in my face.

I take her wrist in my hand and lower it, keeping my eyes on hers as a warning. She's upset, but I don't fucking like the way she's talking to me.

Her breathing is still frantic, but she seems to calm slightly. As she looks at the floor, I take a look at the card.

"Yes," I say and her eyes reach mine and they flash with a knowing look. "Where did you get this?" I ask. My voice is low and threatening, but not toward her. I'm fucking pissed that she had any contact with that snake at all.

"I've been online, I've been searching and searching for the name of the woman you did this to before, but I couldn't find anything."

"What the fuck are you talking about?" Anger makes me push the door open and slam it shut behind me. She takes a step back into her foyer and keeps eye contact.

"He told me you'd done this before." She motions to the card. "You don't know how much it hurt me," she says and her voice cracks and her eyes glass over. The strong suit of armor crumbles into dust and the pain I know she's feeling comes through as her shoulders hunch and her arms wrap around herself. "I couldn't believe you'd do this to me," she says in almost a whisper before wiping the tears from her eyes.

"Never," I say just above a murmur, taking another step forward and slowly pulling her into my chest. "I would never.

I have never done that. I would never do anything to hurt you," I whisper into her hair. Her body is tense and stiff, but after a moment, she relaxes against me.

"He lied to me," she says softly, letting her cheek rest against my hard chest. Although anger is coursing through my blood, holding her in my arms is taming the beast that's pacing inside of me. I'll save my anger for them.

Right now she needs me.

"I don't know what to believe." She speaks so low, I barely hear her. She pulls away slightly, and it cracks a barrier that's kept me from taking her. Her words trigger something in me. A need to prove to her that she's mine. That I would never hurt her.

I take a step forward and then another. Her eyes widen and stare back at me as her back hits the wall of her small apartment foyer.

"I didn't do that to you." There's a hint of anger in my voice. I'm angry that she doesn't trust me. "I didn't set you up and I *will* make him pay for hurting you."

She still seems slightly uncertain and I hate it. "I'll destroy him for what he did to you. He tried to hurt me. Not you. You got caught in the crossfires."

She looks wounded and raw, so full of emotion and I'm not sure which is winning out.

I take her shoulders in my hands to steady her and lower my lips so they're almost touching hers. "You need to trust me, Rose."

Her eyes search my face and her breathing picks up. Her plump lips part and she sinks her teeth into her bottom lip with her eyes on my lips.

It's all I can take.

I crash my lips against hers and cage her small body in.

She instantly melts into me.

"Rose," I say her name reverently and then push her back against the wall, crushing my lips to hers. My dick hardens and presses into her stomach. I'm angry and frustrated, but mostly relieved. I need her. I need her to feel what she means to me.

I pull back, and look down at her.

"I'm sorry, Logan," she says in a hushed voice, staring at me through her thick lashes, willing me to believe her. "I didn't-"

I cut her off, pressing my mouth to hers, my tongue diving into her mouth. My fingers spear through her hair as I kiss her with every bit of passion I have. She pulls away, breathing heavily.

"Please, Logan. You have to know. I'm so sorry. I-"

"Stop." I close my eyes and rest my forehead against hers. "I-" I stop myself before I say words I shouldn't. My chest pangs with pain and I ignore it. I ignore everything and whisper into the hot air between us, "Just let me hold you."

She leans up and presses her body to mine. "I need more," she whispers. My hands roam down to her waist and ass, until I finally pick her up and carry her to her sofa.

I lay her down and kiss the crook of her neck as she

frantically unbuttons my shirt.

"I need you, Logan," she says with shortened breath. "I lo-" I crash my lips to hers and move between her legs, intent on making everything up to her the best way I know how.

I give her all of me. Everything I have.

Even though I know it won't be enough.

CHAPTER 31

CHARLOTTE

*P**lease give me the strength to get through this,* I think to myself as I step out of the Parker-Moore building with Eva.

We're on our way to a press meeting involving the quarterly report of Parker-Moore.

Unfortunately, I've been assigned to answer questions about the new direction of Parker-Moore sales department. Despite not wanting to go, I'm required to be there. It's going to be awful, I just know it. My stomach has been fluttering with butterflies all morning.

Still, not all things have been bad. Yesterday was my first day back at work and no one said anything about the photos, thank God. But people kept coming up and talking to me, making small talk. I knew they were just trying to fish out how I was doing, so it didn't bother me. It did get old after awhile, however.

I hope they'll stop it there, I tell myself as Eva and I climb into the stretch limo that's waiting for us. *Because the constant hovering makes me feel uncomfortable.*

"Are you alright?" Eva asks me as I settle down into the plush leather seats. She's dressed sharper than usual today in a crisp black suit, her hair done up into a single braid down her back, and her makeup is flawless.

I nod my head and say, "Yes, why?"

"You're scowling."

I relax my face muscles. I hadn't even realized that I was doing it. "I just don't want to go to this press meeting. And I think you know why."

Eva gives me a sympathetic look. "I do, but everything will be okay. You have me here. If anyone says *anything* to you about you-know-what, I'll knock them out."

I snort a laugh and she grins at the ridiculousness of what she's said. Eva's not gonna do shit. "Right."

It's silent on the drive over there. Logan's there already. I pick at the hem of my skirt. I wish he was with me now. It's different when he's next to me. It's when I'm alone that the dread and regret and anxiety start to consume me.

"How's things with Logan?" she asks a moment later.

My heart does a flip at his name. I'm honestly kind of

angry with him for wanting to take over the plot to destroy Patterson's company. I'd rather confront the bastard myself and take matters into my own hands. But Logan isn't having it. He wants me to trust him to handle everything. I've agreed... as long as I can stay in contact with the lawyer.

"Good," I answer, letting out an easy breath. "Better than I thought it could be."

Eva smiles and leans over to take my hand. "That's good. I'm happy for you."

And I know that she means it.

Walking into the press room, I'm a ball of nerves. I know people are watching me, judging me. It makes me feel sick to my stomach. Seriously, I'm about to hurl all over Eva's high-dollar suit if I don't get my anxiety under control.

Logan's already on stage taking questions from reporters. I can't get over how professional he looks in his business suit, his hair slicked back. For the first time, he actually looks like who he is. The Boss.

The CEO.

Before I can take my assigned seat on the platform behind the podium, a reporter, a man who looks like he's in his mid-thirties in khaki pants and a plaid shirt, asks, "Mr. Parker, can you tell us how long the affair was with Miss Harrison?"

Anger grips my throat and it's hard to keep a straight face. I knew questions like this would come up, but it's still hard not to react. Eva grips my hand tighter and I walk straight ahead, not looking at the audience and slowly falling into my seat.

I watch as Logan clenches his jaw and I can tell he's trying to keep from blowing a gasket. "I'm not going to answer that question," he responds, his voice tight. "I keep my personal and business life separate, and this press conference is strictly for business."

The man doesn't give up. "But can't you see that what you engaged in is alarming for your company and the stockholders? As head of your company, you should--"

"I said I'm not here to talk about personal matters," Logan says and lowers his voice. "If you don't like it, you can leave." He scans his gaze over the reporters in the room and says, "I will only entertain questions that pertains to Parker-Moore's business dealings."

"But what happened has hurt your company's image," the reporter argues, ignoring Logan's request. "You need to address this issue unless you want to create further damage to your brand."

Logan clenches and unclenches his jaw, anger evident as the veins stand out on his neck. I don't think I ever seen him so angry.

Logan stands there for several moments before saying through gritted teeth, "I'm only going to address this once."

Flashes of photos being taken seem to pick up as Logan responds. My heart beats frantically and I try desperately just to stay in my place, remembering the advice from public relations. "The photos that have been circulated involving myself and Miss Harrison were taken with the intent to hurt myself personally as well as Parker-Moore." He huffs, "A rival of sorts. They can try to slander my name all they want, but what they did was wrong and charges are being pressed. And that's all I'm going to say on this issue."

I hear a mocking laugh in the audience and I scan the crowd to see who it is. I do a double take. It's Patterson. I've seen his picture over and over now that I know who it was that destroyed me without a second thought. He has an evil fucking smirk on his face that makes me want to punch him. "You better watch those accusations, Logan, before you have a lawsuit on your hands. We all know who the 'rival' is that you're talking about, and as far as I know, you have no proof of any wrongdoing on my part."

Logan stands at the podium radiating anger, and the intensity is enough to still my breathing. He stares down Patterson but says nothing. He looks deadly, but Patterson ignores the warning.

"You got caught banging your secretary, and now you're trying to blame me for it... It's obvious you only gave her the job so you could bang her."

I rise from my seat without my own conscious consent and

try to dive for Logan as he climbs off t'

crowd of reporters. He's furious, and he

pumps through my blood and my body

room lets out a collective gasp. His face goin.

tries to scramble over several people to get away from

Logan, but he's too slow. Logan climbs over two people and the metal chairs are tossed out of the way as the crowd disperses, moving away from Logan's target. He grabs Patterson by the collar, yanking him close. I can't see everything, but I can see the first punch. Logan has him on the ground. Fuck! The room erupts into chaos, and the crowd surrounds the two men, shouting and yelling and snapping pictures. I can barely breathe as I push through the crowd.

"Logan!" I yell, my heart beating within my chest like a war drum. There's no way Logan is leaving this room without handcuffs. And even worse, this is going to cause more damage to Parker-Moore than the erotic photos of us ever will. I try to reach him, but I keep getting shoved back. I can't let him do this. I have to stop him.

I'm pushed back against a tide of bodies and am nearly trampled as I stumble off balance. Logan could end up killing Patterson, but all these vultures care about is getting their precious photos to sell to the highest bidder.

"Logan! Stop!" I scream, regaining my balance and trying to push my way through to him. I'm not sure if he heard me, but the crowd parts behind the fight, and I stand as tall as I

⸛ why.

ᴐody and covered in sweat, he begins pushing his ⟋ through the crowd of shouting reporters. He's silent nd heaving in his breaths. Ignoring everyone and heading toward the exit.

Not wasting any time, I chase after him, shoving and pushing my way through anyone that gets in the way.

When I make it outside, there are a crowd of reporters crowding Logan, snapping pictures left and right.

"Logan!" I yell, running in my heels and trying to get his attention. But he doesn't see me, and he doesn't hear me; he's too busy rushing toward the sidewalk where his limo awaits. I watch as Andrew gets out of the vehicle and rushes around to the passenger side, opening the door and holding it open for Logan.

I run as fast as my legs can carry me to the sidewalk, shoving shouting reporters out of the way. I look up, frantically breathing and our eyes meet. Logan gets out and walks straight toward me, pulling me into the limo with him and slamming the door shut. Andrew's already pulling away with screeching tires by the time I'm able to catch my breath and sit up.

"Why did you do that?" I shake my head, practically screaming at him with tears in my eyes. My heart's still pounding. This is bad, it's so fucking bad.

"No one's going to talk to you like that." His voice is weak.

"This isn't good," I say and take in a slow breath, closing

my eyes, trying to calm down.

When Logan doesn't respond, I open my eyes and lean forward, peering at him with concern. It's the first time that I really take a good look at him. His knuckles are bruised and cut, and there's dried blood from his hands up to his arm. It's all over his shirt. I finally reach his face, and my heart stops beating. His eyes seem distant, something... something's wrong. "Logan?"

It takes him a moment to register that I'm talking to him. Logan tries to say something, but his words are unintelligible to my ears and his body sways.

"Logan?" I ask again, panicked now and gripping his shoulders and then head, trying to get him to look at me.

His eyes rolling into the back of his head, Logan collapses against the seat. *Oh my God. No!* "Logan!" I scream, shaking him and refusing to believe this is real. He's unresponsive. I press my hand against his throat.

"What's going on?" Andrew asks with concern.

I scream, "He needs a hospital! Now!"

CHAPTER 32

LOGAN

The constant *beep, beep, beep* from the machine is giving me a fucking headache. I stare at it. The blue and red lines are moving rhythmically across the screen. My back is stiff from being in this fucking hospital bed. The sheets they have are thin and scratchy. My shirt's ripped down the front. They couldn't fucking unbutton it fast enough.

I'm pissed. I don't want to be here.

I'm not ready.

"Mr. Parker?" Doctor Wallace says. I take a deep breath and turn to face him on my right. I school my expression so I don't take the anger out on him. It's not his fault.

It's no one's fault. It just is what it is.

"We need to move this to radiation. It's now stage four non-Hodgkin lymphoma."

I smile weakly and let my head fall to the side.

"The intravenous didn't work then, I take it?" I've been getting intravenous chemotherapy with rituximab every other month for almost two years. At first it was just the pills. Then oral chemo and steroids to reduce the swelling in my spleen and prepare my body for chemotherapy.

I was hoping intravenous every other month would be enough. After all, money can buy the best doctors and good health. Can't it? Apparently not.

"I'm sorry Logan, it's time that we move to the next step. The scan shows that it's moving from the bone, which can be painful."

I huff a humorless laugh. Painful doesn't begin to describe what I felt on that stage. It was like someone stabbing me in my calf, straight to the bone over and over again.

The anger was just barely enough to keep me from acting on the pain. Chadwick Patterson is going to go down for what he did to my Rose. He had the fucking audacity to show up to the conference. That motherfucker. Smashing in his face isn't anywhere close to justice.

I look down at my hand for the first time since I woke up. An IV is sticking out from the back of it, with a thick piece of tape holding it in place.

As I flex my hand it moves slightly, and it's irritating as fuck. There are small cuts on my knuckles that are raw and bruised.

Good. I hope his face looks even worse.

"The radiation is only for twenty-one days and it's user-friendly, so to speak." I look back up to the good doctor and feel slightly sympathetic that I've been ignoring him.

"You'll remain relatively pain free, just tired constantly, and you shouldn't lose your hair," he continues.

"Do I have a choice?" I ask. I don't want radiation. My grandfather died the day they started radiation. He was fine up until then. The slight pain in his chest was the only indication that anything was wrong. I see it as a sign. I don't want it.

"If you want to kill it and live," he says and I look him in the eyes while he gives me a grave expression, "then no, you don't."

I nod my head solemnly, giving in to the inevitable.

A small knock at the door takes the doctor's attention.

He opens it and reveals Charlotte, my Rose. So fragile and beautiful. Yet something I shouldn't hold.

Guilt presses against my chest as I stare into her glassy eyes. Her cheeks are red and tearstained.

Doctor Wallace turns to face me, standing in the doorway to prevent her from coming in farther. "Mr. Park-"

"Yes, let her in." I won't deny her.

She lets out a small sob as she walks into the room.

"Logan," she says and her voice cracks.

"I'm sorry, Rose." She puts a small hand over mine. "I should have told you."

In this moment I hate myself. I know I never had a right

to make her feel anything for me. I was selfish. I'm so fucking undeserving of her.

She shakes her head and doesn't answer me. Instead she grips onto me tighter and tries to calm herself down.

"I still have faith that you'll get through this, Logan," Doctor Wallace says as he opens the door, "I need you to agree to do the radiation though. You have to stop working and work on yourself."

Rose watches as he shuts the door, leaving us alone in the small room.

"I'm sor-" I start to speak, but she interrupts me.

"I talked to the nurses," she says as she goes the corner of the room and drags a chair across the floor and brings it closer to the bed. She flinches and mouths, *sorry* when the leg of the chair scraping along the floor causes a loud scratching sound.

She clears her throat and picks my hand back up. "They said it's curable."

Her eyes move from where our hands are clasped to my eyes. "They said the odds are in your," her voice breaks and she lets go of my hand to cover her face.

Fuck. It breaks my heart to see her like this.

She takes in a ragged but steadying breath and angrily wipes under her eyes.

"Rose, my Rose. I'm so-"

"I'll stay with you." She interrupts me again and takes my hand with both of hers. My lips part and my heart swells. I want so badly to be a selfish prick and not push her away.

But she deserves more.

"I might not make it through this..." A small sob is ripped through her throat again as I press on and say, "You deserve so much more."

She shakes her head and refuses to look at me. She needs to let go. She should just move on with her life. I should've left her alone. This is my fault. "I never should have done this to you." She's quiet for a long moment. My heart is shredded. I don't know how I let this get so out of hand. "You have to go, Charlotte." Her eyes snap up at me at the use of her first name. I have to send her away, it's the right thing to do.

"I won't go, Logan Parker, and you can't make me." She's angry. Furious even. I didn't expect this reaction. I take in a sharp breath and remember the woman I first met. The one who came into my office and was ready to bite my head off for toying with her. "I mean it," she says and her voice takes on a hard edge. "You will not throw me out, Logan."

"It's what's best for you." I try to reason with her.

"I am a grown-ass woman and if I want to stay with you, I'm going to."

My head falls back against the hospital bed. My heart aching and the desire to keep her to myself clouding my judgment. I can't look at her as I say, "Rose-"

"I love you," she says harshly. "I love you, Logan and I'm not going anywhere." My heart does a flip in my chest and I have to stare at her in shock for a moment. I try to comprehend how she could forgive me so easily. She shouldn't. She shouldn't love me either. Not after what I've done to her.

She cups my face and like the selfish man that I am, I lean into her warmth. I open my eyes and stare into hers. There's nothing but love reflecting back at me.

"I'm sorry," I whisper. She kisses me deeply and I reach up to cup the back of her head to deepen it. "I don't deserve you," I say and I know I've never said truer words.

"You don't see yourself clearly." She tells me the words I told her months ago.

I tell her something that's equally true in return. "I love you, my Rose."

CHAPTER 33

CHARLOTTE

"You need to take it easy," I scold Logan, standing over him like a worried hen, my hands on my hips.

It's the second week of Logan's radiation treatments, something that usually leaves him drained and tired, but today he seems to have energy.

The first week was really hard on him, and it seems to be getting better each day. But I can't get over how difficult the first week was. *Today's a new day*, I think, closing my eyes and breathing in deep.

He hasn't needed my help with getting out of bed nor with putting his clothes on. He's even lifted a few things, despite me telling him not to, and hasn't seemed to exhaust himself doing it. Still, I think he should be in bed resting like Doctor Wallace ordered, but he doesn't follow the rules no matter how hard I try to enforce them.

Logan gets what Logan wants. Everything else be damned.

Such thoughts would've turned me on in the past, but now I'm constantly worried. This is his health at stake. He needs to conserve every ounce of energy so he can fight the battle that lies ahead, not use it on work that will be there whenever he's ready to come back to it.

For the past hour I've been trying to get him to get some much needed rest, but he's refused, opting to answer business emails and go over contracts on his laptop instead.

"The company is running fine without you, trust me," I assure him. *If only Logan would relax*, I think to myself, *it would make my job so much easier.*

Since Logan's left the hospital I've become his unofficial nurse, checking up on him and handling all of his immediate needs. It hasn't been easy with his constant desire to keep tabs on Parker-Moore, and it makes me frustrated. His health is more important.

"I'm fine," Logan assures me, tearing his eyes from his laptop screen and looking up at me with a handsome grin. Surprisingly, he looks well rested today and he's sitting in his office chair in just red boxer briefs and no shirt. I must admit, he's a sight for sore eyes, but I'm more concerned with his recovery; it's all I'm concerned about. I let out a heavy sigh and push my hair over my shoulders. My heart feels so heavy.

I'm still having a hard time getting over the shock at finding out he has cancer. He looked so healthy, I never would have suspected he was sick. Just knowing that he's been secretly dealing with this pain all this time makes me want to break down into tears. "I'm just answering these emails and going over some contracts."

I open my lips to argue, but then close them. I know Logan isn't going to listen to me, no matter how much I bitch at him.

Good thing Trent is running the company, I think to myself. *Otherwise, Mr. CEO here would kill himself to make sure everything was working right.*

After he found out the news, Trent offered to take over as CEO until Logan is well enough to work again. To ensure that Logan doesn't try to overwork himself, he's refused to give Logan updates about the company's status and he won't take his calls.

It's pissed Logan off, but it's for his own good.

As far as anyone at the company knows, Logan is on a three-week vacation. There was some gossip back at the company about Logan going to jail, but after Patterson was arrested and plead guilty to the charges after seeing the evidence against him, that all stopped.

"You need to stop worrying about me," Logan scolds me, seeing my concerned expression. "You're only going to stress yourself out. And I don't want that."

"Well that's not happening," I tell him firmly. I hate how casual he is about brushing off my concerns. I think he does it to hide his worry and put me at ease, but he doesn't have to. I don't want him to either. I'm here for him. All of him. I wish he would confide in me more. "I'm going to worry whether you like it or not, thank you very much."

Logan cocks an eyebrow and sits back in his chair. Desire stirs within me, seeing his six-pack abs that seem even more well-defined these days. He's lost some weight from being sick in the hospital, maybe five pounds, but he still looks the same, still devastatingly handsome. And the sight of him brings the part of me that needs his comforting touch to the forefront. "Oh yeah?" he asks.

"Yeah."

"Come here," he says and pats his lap, scooting the chair out from his desk. I hesitate for a moment, wondering if it's prudent to sit on him, but I can't deny the urge. For a full week, sex and even the idea of sex have been nonexistent. Worry and fear were a constant, but things are different now. And I love it when he holds me. Right now, I need him to soothe my pain. Even if that makes me selfish.

Wrapping my arms around his neck, I nestle into his lap as he spears his fingers through my hair. He looks up at me with an intensity that makes shivers run down my neck and arms. "You're so fucking beautiful, you know that?"

My cheeks heat at his praise and warmth flows through

my chest at his words. "Stop it."

Logan shakes his head. "No," he begins and there's strength in his words I don't expect, "the day I met you was the luckiest day of my life." He gently rubs his nose against mine and says, "You saved me."

Tears prick my eyes and begin rolling down my face. "I love you," I whisper, my heart aching. I tell him that as often as I can. If nothing else, I need him to know how much I truly love him. I wipe the tears from my eyes and try to stop being so emotional.

"And I love you too, my beautiful Rose." He pulls me down against him, pressing his lips against mine. I kiss him back with all the passion I have, pushing myself into him. His hands roam down my body and I groan at the sensation. It feels amazing to be touched by him again. Beneath me, I can feel his hard cock against my ass, pulsating and throbbing. I want him, and I moan into his kiss at the thought. I *need* him. Now.

We shouldn't be doing this, I tell myself, but I don't push him away. I gasp as he pinches my nipple, which sends a throbbing need to my clit. He groans into my mouth as his hand travels up my shirt. *Logan should be resting and recovering.* But it feels so right. And I want him just as much as he wants me.

He's in the process of undoing my bra when there's a knock at the door. Startled and breathless, I jump out of his lap and start smoothing out my outfit.

Shit. I forgot Doctor Wallace was stopping by. I try to

smooth out my hair and calm myself down as Logan smirks at me and rises out of the chair. I watch as he repositions himself inside his boxers to make his erection less obvious before he goes over to answer the door.

The lust I was feeling moments ago floods out of me as Doctor Wallace walks into the room carrying a large black bag, and I'm filled with anxiety.

"Good afternoon," the doctor greets me with a smile that makes me even more nervous.

"Good afternoon, Doctor Wallace," I barely say above a murmur as I respectfully give him a wide berth, taking a seat in the corner of the room.

The doctor gives me a tight smile and says, "Just checking in on Mr. Parker here." He sets his bag down on Logan's desk, and I stare at it numbly, hating it. Hating that Logan has to go through this, hating that he's sick at all. I clench my fists with anger thinking about it.

I need to think happy thoughts and stay positive. But it's hard. Logan's outlook looks bleak. Stage four. Who beats that? My heart squeezes in my chest and I have to close my eyes to keep the tears from sliding out. I just want him healthy.

Doctor Wallace begins his physical examination that I've seen a few times now, checking Logan's vital signs, shining a light into his eyes and performing an oral examination. All the questions are the same. This isn't the first time I've seen the examination, but I listen just as closely, and my heart slows all the same. Every second feels like a lifetime. I just need him to be okay.

"Everything seems to be as expected, Mr. Parker," Doctor Wallace says when he's done with his diagnostics. "Well, you're doing better than I expected you would at this stage." He sits back with a nod and says, "That's a good sign."

The doctor's words are soothing, but it's still hard to have hope. Just because Logan appears to be doing okay, doesn't mean anything if the cancer is still there.

I pray that it only gets better from here. It has to. It better. "It does?" Logan lets out a deep breath and says, "Good."

Doctor Wallace nods. "It does indeed." He looks around and scratches his nose. "Actually, I thought you'd be in bed like I told you."

Logan grins over at me. "It's hard to lie there and sleep when I have such a beautiful woman to keep me company."

The doctor chuckles, and a fierce blush comes over my cheeks. It's cute, but I know Logan is worried just as much as I am deep down. I want to laugh and pretend that everything is okay, but I can't. This cuts too deep.

"What happens after this?" I ask concernedly.

Doctor Wallace turns to look at me. "We continue the treatments everyday so long as Logan feels well enough, until it's gone." He looks back at Logan and pats him on the shoulder. "If it gets to be too much, we can take a break and see how you recover." His voice is somber, and it makes my heart clench.

I suck in a painful breath, my heart feeling like it's being crushed. I wish there were something I could do to cure Logan, to take his pain away.

Fuck cancer, I think to myself angrily, fighting back the sea of tears. *Logan doesn't deserve this shit.*

"I'll see you tomorrow, Logan," Doctor Wallace replies, rising to his feet and gathering his instruments into his black bag.

Bidding us farewell, Doctor Wallace turns to leave the room, but before he can walk out, I stop him at the door.

"Is he really going to be alright?" I ask him quietly. I hate asking him this, and I feel somewhat confrontational, but I can't let him leave me with a sense of false hope. I don't want to think Logan is going to be okay if he's not. "Please, don't sugarcoat it. I want the one hundred percent truth."

Doctor Wallace gives me a sad smile and places a firm hand on my shoulder. "As much as I would love to be able to ease your worries, Charlotte, I can't give you a definite answer. The treatments we're using have worked many times for my patients, and Logan's condition today is a good sign. But I can't give you anything definitive. Will Logan be alright? Only God knows that."

The doctor leaves, and I close the door behind him. Feeling a bit weak, I lean against the door for support, my forehead pressed against the hard wood.

Behind me I hear footsteps, and then I feel strong arms wrapping around my waist. I can't help but melt into his embrace.

"Stop worrying, Rose," Logan whispers in my ear before delivering a small kiss to my neck. "I'll be alright. You heard the man." He's trying to inject strength in his voice, to soothe me, but I can still sense the uncertainty hiding in his words. The pain.

Fuck. It hurts. "I'll try not to," I say over the lump in my throat. I turn to face him, fighting back the tears and look into his face. "I just love you so much and want to see you get through this."

Logan squeezes me as tight as his diminished strength allows and returns my kiss. "I promise you, my Rose, I won't stop fighting. If there is any chance of me beating this thing, I'm going to fucking do it. For myself, but most of all, for you."

The tears can't be denied, they flow down my face in a torrent and I collapse against Logan, sobbing. Fuck this. Fuck life. Fuck everything.

"I need you to be strong for me, Rose," Logan urges me, kissing my hair and rocking me gently. "Everything's going to be okay, and even if it's not, I'll always be here for you." I cry harder, big hiccuping sobs, until I'm gasping for breath. Logan continues to rock me, comforting me, holding me, loving me, until I'm all cried out.

"I'm so sorry," I lament when it's over, sniffling and wiping at my nose. I feel slightly embarrassed. Breaking down like that isn't going to make anything better. But I needed to get that out since I've been holding the pain inside for days now.

"You're right. I need to be strong."

He rests his forehead against mine and says, "You are strong, my Rose." He kisses me sweetly and I mold my body to his. He takes my hand in his and raises it above my head, all the while kissing me. But it's awkward, it feels weird and I don't know what he's doing. I break the kiss and look up as he's slipping a golden engagement ring sparkling against the light onto my ring finger.

My heart stops in my chest and my mouth falls open. He releases my hand and pulls back slightly. *A ring.* I stare at my hand in disbelief.

"Oh my God," I gasp, clutching my hand to my chest as my heart skips a beat. Ordinarily, something like this would have sent me through the roof, but I feel like I've been punched in the stomach.

The tears are back, and I fucking hate it. I'm two seconds away from being a blubbering mess again and it's for all the wrong reasons.

"Marry me, Rose," Logan implores, his heart in his eyes. It tears at me. He can see my pain, and I can see his. "Marry me tonight." He pauses and says, "Or tomorrow at the latest."

I open my mouth to speak, but no words come out. This should be the happiest moment of my life. I should be jumping up and down with joy, yet all I can feel is a heavy, crushing pain that refuses to get the fuck off my chest.

The heavy feeling is compounded by the knowledge of

why Logan wants me to marry him tonight.

Because he knows he might not be here tomorrow.

The thought is nearly enough to bring me to my knees and I sway like a leaf in the wind. Logan catches me before I can fall, and I hate myself for it. Here I am falling to pieces, when I should be strong for him. For us both. Logan continues the assault on my heart, though I know he doesn't mean to. "If something happens to me, I want you to have everything. The business, all my assets. Everything."

I shake my head, feeling like I'm being suffocated. "No, Logan. I refuse to accept it, and I don't- I can't marry you for that... That's not-" I shake my head, unable to accept this and unable to talk and my heart tries to leap up my throat. I can't take the thought of him dying. I can't bear it.

Logan continues to hold me tight and it breaks my heart because I know he's using what little strength he has to hold onto me. "I want you to marry me because I fucking love you."

The pain is surreal. I'm so choked up that it's hard to breathe, much less get out words. "Logan..." I croak.

Logan pulls me in tighter, kissing the tears staining my face. "Just tell me yes, Rose. I *need* this. Don't deny me, my Rose." He squeezes me weakly.

My words are choked and reflect the pain I'm in as I stare into his loving gaze. "Only if you promise to never leave me," I whisper, barely hanging on by a thread. I know it's a promise that Logan has no way of knowing he can keep, but I want it anyway.

Logan hesitates and it sends a sharp pain into my heart. In this moment, a promise is a hollow thing. We both know it. But I need to hear it. I need something to hold on to. "I'll do my best," Logan finally replies, and it doesn't make me feel any better. "I'll stick around forever... or for as long as I'm able to fight."

I can't take anymore.

Feeling like my heart is going to explode, I collapse against him and sob into his chest until I'm all spent.

Over and over I tell him, "I love you, Logan." I plead with him, "Don't leave me."

"I love you, my Rose," he says softly and with a sincerity I can't deny.

CHAPTER 34

LOGAN

"This is where he lives?" my Rose asks me as she slips out of the car. I have my hand held out for her, and although she rests her small hand in mine, she doesn't put her weight in it. I wish she would. I wish she wouldn't walk on eggshells around me.

It was better when I'd kept it hidden. When she didn't know about the cancer, and was blissfully unaware.

Things are different between us, and in some ways I hate it. Like this moment, when she didn't even want me to drive. Others are sweeter now that her walls have fallen down and she doesn't hide a thing from me. Those moments make it all worth it.

I stretch out and even though it's brisk in the early morning, the chill feels refreshing.

"Yes, it's been... nearly seven years now." I answer her question as she takes in the ancient stone building. I shell out a pretty penny for my father to live here, but it's the best service and quality that any place has to offer for him in his state.

My heart pains in my chest at the thought; I almost had myself admitted to a similar environment.

I close the door with a heavy heart as Rose's heels click on the sidewalk and a breeze lifts the dried leaves off the ground, causing a soft rustling to fill my senses.

My body did not take the first week of radiation well. I was constantly nauseated and fatigued. And worried that the inevitable was going to happen. I wanted to send Rose away. I did try though, several times, and had I been well, she would have beat the shit out of me.

Five days on and two days off. That weekend I recovered well and Rose stayed by my side the entire time and told me to fuck off when I tried to send her away.

The thought brings a smile to my lips as I look up and watch her walking up the rough stone stairs of the building in her heels. She's gripping the railing and I'm quick to make my way over and hold her waist, helping her to balance.

She smiles sweetly, the chill making her cheeks flush a beautiful shade of pink. Her engagement band clinks on the metal railing as we walk up together, and the sound fills me with pride.

She's my wife.

I've never been so proud. I have yet to tell my father though, and Rose hasn't told a soul.

Legally we're married, but as far as everyone else knows, we're engaged.

She wants it to stay that way.

I open the door for her and she looks at me with exasperation. It's a heavy door and just climbing those stairs took a lot out of me, but I'm not going to just stay in bed everyday until I die. I want to be me. I want to live my life, and that includes opening doors for my wife.

It hurts me that she doesn't want to tell people. At first I thought she was ashamed. But she's scared of what they'll think.

She doesn't want the will changed either, but she has no fucking choice in that matter. That's already been done.

The warmth of the building cocoons us as we walk in. The front hall is open and spacious.

The deep red oriental runner placed down along the length of the hall muffles the sound of Rose's steps as we move from the stone floors to the rug.

She slips her coat easily off her shoulders and I move to take it. She looks up at me with worried eyes.

"It's only a coat, Rose; I think I can manage." There's a hint of admonishment in my tone and she purses her lips. She doesn't argue though, she doesn't like to as much now, knowing that I'm not well.

An asymmetric grin pulls to my lips at the thought; that is one benefit of being ill, I suppose.

"Logan," I hear my father's rough voice call out to me from the sunroom to our left, before we make it to the welcome desk. I lead Rose, splaying my hand on her back.

The sunroom has several tables and comfortable chairs. The stone fireplace is lit, and the heat feels welcoming.

As we get closer, I notice how my father's eyes are solely on Rose. She's walking a bit slower with her hands clasped in front of her.

Anger stirs in my chest.

I didn't bring her here for him to make her uncomfortable.

I wanted them to meet at least once, just in case, but I won't let him make her feel unwelcome. She's my bride, my wife, the love of my life. And he had better realize that and respect it, or we're going to have problems.

"Mr. Parker," Rose says in a professional tone I recognize from all of our meetings and presentations. She has an amazing ability to slip into a mask of ease when she's uncomfortable. I fucking hate it.

"Father, meet my wife, Charlotte Rose." I introduce them while staring hard into my father's pale blue eyes. They widen slightly, and his mouth falls open with surprise.

"Wife?" he asks with raised brows. Before I can answer he replies with disbelief, "I never thought I'd live to see the day."

He looks at her stomach before reaching Rose's eyes.

My face heats with embarrassment. I don't want him to think I've knocked her up, although the thought makes my dick stir in my slacks.

"Fiancé he means," Rose is quick to reply smoothly, and my father's eyes dart to her ring finger before he nods his head easily, sitting back in his seat.

He's confirming her fears and I fucking hate it, although I suppose I can see his position.

"I see my son has been keeping secrets," he says as he eyes me and then holds out a hand for Rose. "At least he introduced us before you two tied the knot."

Their handshake is business at best, but Rose seems comforted by the warmer reception.

I take a seat, my body stiff as the anxiety of the two of them getting along grows.

"How did you two meet?" he asks Rose.

She smiles warmly, tucking a strand of hair behind her ear. She looks hesitantly at me and then leans forward and replies, "At a conference a few months ago."

My father nods, and then a smile suddenly appears at his lips. He raises his hand, pointing at her and nodding his head as he says, "Don't tell me, you worked for..." he snaps his fingers and my heartbeat picks up. "Armcorp?" he asks.

Rose's beautiful smile grows across her face as she asks, "He told you?" Her brow furrows, although she looks pleased.

"Not exactly, but I had a feeling."

I huff a humorless laugh. My father has always struck me as intelligent, but I didn't think I was so obvious.

I sit back in my chair as the two of them engage in easy conversation.

My leg pains me again, reminding me that I have radiation again tomorrow. One more week, and then we'll see where I stand.

I ignore the pain and smile along with Rose's story of how I ruined her presentation.

She laughs and pauses to remember the rest of our story. I remember it, though I don't know if I remember it as clearly as Rose.

My father interrupts before she's able to continue, saying, "I'm proud of you son," and his voice cracks. He clears his throat and adds, looking back at Rose, "I'm happy for the two of you. I'm happy he found someone to love."

"Thank you," Rose says with a soft voice. I can tell she wasn't expecting it. I wasn't either.

My father and I exchange a silent nod. My heart is swelling in my chest at his approval. This is what I wanted. I wasn't sure if he'd understand. But it means the world to me that he does.

Rose nervously clears her throat and picks up from where she left off. Her hands wave in the air as she talks about how she was so nervous to meet her new boss.

My father's not watching her though, he's watching me. His eyes are filled with pride and glassy with tears.

I've never seen him so emotional before. Not since the day I told him I had cancer, although back then he was in disbelief. Now, his happiness is evident. It brings a warmth to my chest.

I can only hope I live to see the day that she proudly calls me her husband. I unconsciously take her hand in mine and kiss her wrist.

It makes her pause her story and her eyes soften with happiness, although her cheeks flush with a blush of embarrassment.

"I love you," I tell her easily.

"Logan," she says shyly, looking between myself and my father.

"Don't deny me, my Rose."

I can see her blossom with love shining in her eyes as she whispers, "I love you, too."

I know she does.

Epilogue

Logan

Remission is a beautiful word.

I'm still on edge most days, thinking the cancer will come back. But it's been a year and the scans show no visible signs of returning.

"Logan!" I hear Rose's voice from the other side of the penthouse.

The large doors are open and it lets in a cool breeze. It's getting late and I should shut them, but I can see the ocean from here and the palm trees are close enough to touch. It's a beautiful escape from the city, and our first night here. I was nearly asleep on the sofa, lost in work as usual. But it was only for tonight to wrap up a meeting I couldn't put off. And then no computer. Charlotte's orders.

I put the laptop on the coffee table, sliding it across the glass and stand up. Stretching out my sore muscles.

I crack my neck and sigh. It was a long ride on the jet. Nearly six hours. I shouldn't complain, after all, it was a jet, but I fucking hate traveling. You'd think I'd be used to it by now, but I'm not. I'm not sure I ever will be either.

"Logan," my Rose calls out again.

I take large strides to where her voice came from, the bedroom suite.

She's standing in front of the dresser, putting away the clothes from her suitcase. I don't know why she does these things, there's hired help here to do just that. But she always insists on doing it herself.

She bends down to put away whatever's in her hand into the bottom drawer. Her pale pink cotton dress slips up her thighs and just barely shows the curves of her ass. I have to suppress a groan of satisfaction. I fucking love that ass. I love every bit of her.

"Yes, my bride?" I ask her as I walk up behind her and wrap my arms around her waist, pulling her back into my chest. Her lush ass pushes against my cock and it already starts hardening for her. I want her now even more than I did when we first met. I have no plans for that to ever change.

She rolls her eyes and scoffs. "Just because we're on our honeymoon doesn't mean I'm your bride." She lays back in my arms and gives me a sweet smile as her baby blues find mine in the mirror.

I chuckle and hold her closer to me, loving her warmth.

"And whose fault is that?" I ask her. We've been married for nearly three months now, legally six, but my Rose insists on ignoring the online certificate. She didn't even wear the wedding band I picked out for her until we had the *real* ceremony.

Charlotte was so caught up in her work that she wasn't ready to take so much time off for a honeymoon. She's finally got the entire department running smoothly. She's always been good at what she does, and it makes me damn proud. I hadn't anticipated her being as much of a workaholic as I am though. Thankfully, we've started slowing down and hiring more people so we can do less.

It's time to enjoy life. I have one worth living, with a partner I want to enjoy.

"I was thinking..." I stare at her reflection in the mirror, but her eyes don't meet mine. She busies herself with folding a shirt that's on top of the dresser.

"What were you thinking, my Rose?" I ask gently, planting a small kiss on her neck.

She hums sweetly and leans her head against my shoulder with her eyes closed.

Her small, delicate hands find mine on her waist and she slowly opens her eyes to stare back at me in the mirror. "I was wondering," her eyes dart down, then back to me, "if we could make this a babymoon?"

My eyebrows raise comically as she says the word I assumed I'd be hearing on this little vacation of ours. Her friend Eva's recently gotten pregnant. Ever since she announced it, Charlotte has been all about babies and pregnancies.

She's more than hinted. And I'm taking it seriously.

My brow furrows. ...wait.

"A babymoon?" I ask her, "Isn't that for when you're already pregnant?"

She nods her head with a twinkle in her eye.

Oh, shit. My grip on her loosens as my mouth opens.

"Oh no!" she says as she bends over slightly with a wide smile. She covers her face as she laughs at me. "No, no, not yet." She turns in my arms and I let out a breath I didn't know I was holding.

My heart slams in my chest and I close my eyes to try to calm down.

I guess I'm not quite as ready as I thought I was.

She places her hand on my chest and fiddles with the buttons on my dress shirt.

"I just meant, we could try. We have two full weeks." She stands on her tiptoes and plants a small kiss on my lips.

I close my eyes, enjoying her touch. I love this woman so damn much.

I live for her. Only for her.

She pulls away slightly and when I open my eyes, she's

looking up at me through her thick lashes with hope.

I grin at her. "I think we can try."

"Ah!" Her high-pitched shriek makes me close my eyes. She jumps up and down and wraps her arms around my neck, practically swinging.

I laugh and look down at the beautiful smile on her face.

I'll do everything I can to make her happy. And if that means we're going to have a baby, then I'll be the best father I can. Our children will never go without.

"I love you so much, Logan," she says before kissing me passionately.

I break our kiss, only to tell her what I've said every single day since I first confessed it, "I love you, my Rose."

ABOUT THE AUTHORS

Thank you so much for reading our co-written novel. We hope you loved reading it as much as we loved writing it!

For more information on the books we have published, bonus scenes and more visit our websites.

More by Willow Winters
www.willowwinterswrites.com/books

More by Lauren Landish
www.laurenlandish.com

CPSIA information can be obtained
at www.ICGtesting.com
Printed in the USA
LVHW110942290822
726699LV00001B/10